A BYRN...

SECRET
Sin

❀ Created with Vellum

Books by Jill Ramsower

The Byrne Brothers Series
Silent Vows
Secret Sin (Novella)
Corrupted Union

The Five Families Series
Forever Lies
Never Truth
Blood Always
Where Loyalties Lie
Impossible Odds
Absolute Silence
Perfect Enemies

The Savage Pride Duet
Savage Pride
Silent Prejudice

The Of Myth & Man Series
Curse & Craving
Venom & Vice
Blood & Breath
Siege & Seduction

SECRET SIN

A BYRNE BROTHERS NOVELLA

JILL RAMSOWER

To all the accomplished, generous, intelligent ladies out there who simply want a man with a filthy, filthy mouth.

ONE

TEQUILA COULD REALLY MAKE A GIRL'S HEAD SPIN. OR
maybe that was just the result of learning my uncle had
killed his wife. The news had certainly thrown me for a
loop.

In the months since my aunt's death, life had felt
frozen in some kind of supernatural time warp. My
cousin, who also happened to be my best friend in the
world, had lost her voice and wouldn't leave her house.
Our entire family tree was shrouded in grief. Life
slowed to a standstill until everything launched back
into motion one day, skipping straight past normal and

into hyper speed. It was so disorienting that my head spun.

I looked at my warped reflection in the brushed metal doors of the elevator and bit back a giggle.

Yeah, tequila was definitely playing its part.

Noemi and I had downed shots of Patrón while she'd told me the truth about her mother's death. She'd kept it secret for months, and it felt incredible to remove that barrier between us. To finally be moving forward.

"Day drinking?" Bishop's voice greeted me as soon as the elevator doors opened.

I smirked at a twin set of dimples that were too cute to be legal.

"I'm an adult," I quipped back.

"Last time I checked, twenty was still a year shy of the legal drinking age in New York."

"Like that ever stopped *you*." I hadn't known Bishop long, but we'd spent hours together at Noemi's wedding days before, and I knew the carefree playboy wasn't the sort to bother with rules. He and I had toyed with an electric chemistry that sizzled between us, dancing precariously on the edge of a dangerous cliff.

With excitement and alcohol thrumming in my veins, I felt propelled right back to that precipice at the sight of the beautiful Irishman. If his loosely cut mahogany curls and glinting brown eyes didn't make a girl weak in the knees, his square-cut jawline and epic dimples were bound to strike a killing blow. And that was just his face. Bishop's perfectly chiseled body would have made Michelangelo weep. Hell, I may have shed a tear or two thinking about him.

Bishop, whose real name I'd learned was actually Ewan Bohanan, carried himself with a kind of easygoing confidence so potent it had its own gravitational pull. He was playful, intensely masculine, and devastatingly gorgeous. He was also here to take me home from my cousin's place, and I was entirely too tipsy to behave.

He grinned and leaned closer. "Yeah, but I do all sorts of things you shouldn't."

I inched forward, looking up at him through my lashes. "Shame on you, Mr. Bohanan," I purred. "Don't you know this is the twenty-first century? Women can do anything men can do."

"Not sure your father would agree."

"Never stopped me before." Lies. Dad had gotten in the way plenty over the years, but I was taking control now. I'd already started secretly searching for my own apartment. I had a whole list of Things Independent Women Do, and Bishop Bohanan suddenly looked like a perfect chance to tick off another item from the list.

Have a crazy-hot one-night stand.

This situation was ideal. Dad's driver had dropped me off at Noemi's before lunch, and I wouldn't be expected home until dinner. Bishop was hot, unattached, and familiar enough that he wasn't a total stranger. I couldn't have asked for a better setup.

The direction of my thoughts must have shown on my face because his smile evaporated and was replaced with something dark and lusty. "I think it's time to get you home before things get carried away." His voice dropped to a gravelly rumble that stoked a heat deep in my belly. My breathing hitched, drawing his eyes to my lips. With a tortured groan, he spun me toward the building entrance. "Start walking, and don't look at me like that." Temptation gnawed at his self-control. Good. I liked the idea of Bishop mindless with need, unable to think clearly.

I reluctantly obliged, one of his hands pressing me forward like a gun at my back. A smirk teased at my lips as he led me to a bright-yellow Mustang that suited his vibrant personality perfectly.

"Your car is gorgeous."

"Thanks. You're not going to throw up in it, are you?"

I shot a glare at him over my shoulder. "If you don't know the difference between tipsy and trashed, maybe I misjudged you." I turned and leaned against his car, facing him with a challenging stare.

"I'm exactly who you think I am." His drastic shift from playful ease to lethal intensity was impressive.

Listening to Noemi tell her story over the past hour had lit a fire inside me. While our fathers were very different—mine had never threatened my life like hers had—I still felt compelled to follow my father's orders. An arranged marriage for me was in the realm of possibilities, and two weeks was all the warning Noemi had been given.

That could have been me.

I didn't like the idea of being tied to a man I hardly

knew, but if I had no choice, I would be damned if I didn't at least experience life first. So far, my experience with men was shamefully limited. No boy at school would go anywhere near me—Dad made sure of that. And when Aunt Nora died and Noemi withdrew, going out and having fun just didn't seem right. I'd been stuck in a sort of lockdown almost as much as Noemi. It was time to shake off the stupor and start living.

My breath caught in my throat as my hand extended to clasp the front of his shirt with a gentle tug. "Then prove it. Take me to your place."

Bishop's nostrils flared while the rest of his body hardened to chiseled granite.

Not wanting him to see me as an inexperienced little girl, I pulled him closer until his body came into full contact with mine. "You're overthinking this, stud. We've been dancing around one another since we met. Time to let this run its course." I could hardly believe the confident words falling from my lips. I sounded like one badass, self-assured modern woman, and the thrill was just as intoxicating as the tequila still warming my veins.

"Fuck," he hissed. "You're trying to get me killed, aren't you?"

"Don't flatter yourself. It's not like you're getting away with some monumental crime."

Grabbing my hand, he pulled me around to the passenger side and held open the door. "Get in."

Checkmate.

5

WE ONLY MADE it a few steps into Bishop's tenth-floor apartment before he had my back against a wall, hand cuffing my throat while his lips devoured mine.

He didn't just kiss me. He lay siege and conquered, all while humming a voracious groan. I was more than happy to concede defeat. My hands mindlessly tugged at his shirt, desperately needing to strip away the barriers between us. It didn't matter that I'd never done this before. Everything about being with Bishop felt natural and right, like singing a song I'd known from birth.

He broke away long enough to yank his shirt over his head while I did the same, grateful I'd worn a sexy hot-pink bra that made the most of my modest curves.

"*Fuck.*" His eyes glazed over as he took me in. "You're even better than I'd imagined."

I continued to undress, unbuttoning my jean shorts and letting them drop to the floor. Bishop hooked a thumb in the cup of my bra and swiftly freed my breast before taking the taut peak in his mouth. Electric need seared a path from my nipple down to my clit, a surge of blood flow pulsing in the delicate bundle of nerves. My head dropped back against the wall, and my lips parted in a sigh of pure ecstasy.

"*Bishop,*" I breathed, my fingers weaving into his silky curls. "You ... imagined ... being with me?" I murmured past the intoxicating sensations overwhelming my body.

"For the past two nights, I've pictured your soft curves while I fucked my hand raw."

God, I loved his unabashed honesty. I hadn't thought

he could get any sexier, but every word out of his mouth only added to my tsunami of desire.

"And what about this mouth?" I asked coyly, gliding my tongue across my bottom lip. "Did you picture my mouth doing dirty things to you in these fantasies of yours?" I dropped to my knees before he could answer and unfastened his pants, my eyes glued to his the entire time.

I didn't know who this goddess was that had taken over me, but I adored everything about her. I felt like I'd unlocked a new version of myself. Someone powerful and bold. A woman who knew what she wanted and wasn't afraid to take it. Pippa 2.0 Boss Bitch and Goddess Extraordinaire.

Bishop's entire body shuddered with restraint.

"The things I want to do to that mouth would send me straight to hell." His ragged voice caressed my bare skin, spurring me onward.

When his heavy cock spilled free from his boxers, I had to push aside the staggering need to gape at his masculine beauty. I'd never seen a dick up close and certainly never dreamed it would be so damn mesmerizing. The throbbing heat. The veins bulging down his impressive length. The velvety texture of his skin so soft when compared to the impossible hardness within.

He was a goddamn work of art, and I wanted to appreciate every square inch of him, but I didn't want him to know I was a virgin. Twice before, I'd had guys bow out at the last second when I told them the truth.

How the hell was I ever going to give up my v-card if no one was willing to man up? Not this time. I wouldn't give him any reason to doubt me, and what he didn't know wouldn't hurt him.

I clasped my hand around his base and sucked the salty head of his cock into my mouth. I savored the feel of his scalding heat against my tongue with several swipes around the tip. Eager to test myself, I took in a lungful of air, flattened my tongue, then sucked him deep to the back of my throat.

"*Christ*, kitten. You suck me off like a fuckin' champ."

I peered up in time to see his head fall back, his hand cupping the back of my head. His praise lit my insides with a flood of radiant light. I'd never imagined it could feel so good to pleasure a man, but watching him come undone at my touch was better than any drug.

I bobbed my head, licking and sucking like his dick was an icicle and I hadn't had water in days. When I moaned with him deep in my throat, he pulled my head back and groaned.

"Enough. The first time I come in you will be in that sweet pink pussy." He helped me to my feet, then wrenched my panties down to my ankles. Anticipation bubbled like expensive champagne under my skin as he pulled a condom package from his wallet and ripped it open. Once he was fully sheathed, he pinned me with a stare so damn primal that my knees threatened to give out.

"I need you inside me, Bishop." I hoped he attributed my breathiness to need rather than nerves. I *was* ready

8

for him, but I was anxious, too. I had to make sure not to give away any discomfort. If I acted normal, and he was sufficiently in the moment, I was confident he'd never suspect what I'd done. Men weren't exactly the most observant of creatures at the best of times.

"You ready for me, baby?" He cupped one hand around the back of my neck to guide my lips to his while his other hand slid deftly between my folds. A rumble clawed its way from his chest. "So fucking wet already. Come here." He lifted me into his arms and pressed my back against the wall with my legs wrapped tight around his waist.

This was it. The moment I shed that damn virgin label and strode confidently into womanhood.

A triumphant grin crept across my face before I slammed my lips on his in the same instant Bishop thrust inside me.

I did it! And I didn't even wince, even though that shit hurt!

I was so caught up in my own elation and dizzying emotions that it took me a second to realize Bishop had gone inhumanly still.

"What.

"The.

"*Fuck.*"

Each savage word punctured the tension-filled air around us with lethal precision.

Bishop slowly brought his blistering stare to mine.

Oh shit.

Oh shit. Oh shit. Oh shit.

This was not going how I'd planned. He knew. He knew exactly what I'd done, and he was livid.

"It's okay, Bishop. I wanted this. I promise." I tried to reassure him.

"And what about me, Pippa?" he barked. "Did you stop to think about whether *I* wanted this?"

Ouch.

The sexual siren inside me shriveled up like the poor souls in *The Little Mermaid* after striking a deal with the evil sea witch.

I lowered my feet, wincing as he slid out of me, and kept my eyes cast downward. I'd been so eager to finally know what it felt like to be with a man that I hadn't considered the consequences if I'd been wrong. Bishop's disgust bathed me in a sticky coating of shame.

"Fuck, that's not what I meant," he grumbled. "That's not how it should have happened, Pippa. Your first time shouldn't be up against a goddamn wall." He raked a hand through his hair and scanned the room as if searching for answers. "Fuck it. No going back now, so I might as well do this right." He grabbed my hand and pulled me back to his bedroom.

I tried not to feel like a misbehaving child, but it was hard not to. I'd deceived him, and I knew it. Guilt somehow whitewashed over every ounce of courage I'd felt minutes earlier, leaving me vulnerable and uncertain.

We stopped at the foot of his masculine king-sized bed. His room was comfortable, even if a little messy. A few pieces of laundry dotted the floor, and his bed wasn't made, but all the furnishings were expensive, and the décor cohesive. It was refined but lived in. I liked it. A lot.

Bishop faced me and brought a finger up under my bra strap, slowly drifting his touch down to the top of my breast. "How could someone so fucking incredible have never been touched before?"

His question was rhetorical since all of his attention focused on the movement of his fingers. I couldn't have responded had I wanted to. The intensity of his words and mesmerizing feel of his touch rendered me speechless.

Bishop reached behind me to unclasp my bra—the last article of clothing between us. He didn't immediately slip it off me. Instead, he brought his fingers up to the thin straps on my shoulders and teased them downward, his hungry stare fixed on each sliver of newly revealed skin until gravity took hold, and the lace fell to the floor.

My nipples puckered impossibly tighter. Breaths grew shallow.

I felt so much more exposed than I had before, and it had nothing to do with my clothes. Everything about this felt different than it had when we'd first entered the apartment. Our sultry playfulness had morphed into something infinitely more poignant. The air itself felt saturated with emotion, and I wasn't sure if I wanted to breathe it in or run for the nearest exit.

"I should tan your ass for pulling a stunt like this, but I suppose you've been punished enough." His eyes lifted to mine, finally softening a fraction. "Are you in any pain?"

I shook my head. "Not anymore."

He nodded once, then cut his eyes to the bed. "On your back."

I did as he instructed but hesitated when he lowered himself and motioned for me to spread my knees.

"I'm not sure you want to do that. I may have bled a little."

Hands on my knees, he opened me wide. "If I didn't want to do this, I wouldn't." His lips kissed my inner thigh, working slowly higher with nips and licks that brought a fire raging to life in my belly. "Tell me you've at least played with yourself before."

"Yes. I'm not a prude, just overprotected."

Teeth nipped at my outer lip for my smart response.

I gasped, my inner muscles clenching tight. "Please, touch me. I need you to touch me," I panted.

"I'm getting there, kitten. You can't rush these things." Bishop slid a finger inside me. I was more sore than I'd realized, but when he hooked that finger to tap at a spot inside me, the pleasure already simmering in my veins magnified tenfold.

I moaned. Loudly.

"Jesus, it feels so good." I'd had orgasms before, but this was different. With Bishop's fingers stirring up a fire inside me, my body quivered and quaked with the impending threat of a tidal wave of pleasure. When he finally sucked on my clit, stimulating the swollen bundle of nerves, the wave crashed over me so thoroughly that I lost all control. A cry of pure bliss clawed its way from my throat. My body convulsed, and I was pretty sure my soul momentarily left my body.

As I recovered, Bishop covered my body with his, then kissed me deeply.

"Taste yourself on my tongue, kitten. *Now* you're ready." He raised my knees back and nudged himself an inch inside me.

I felt an odd emptiness after my orgasm. Like my body knew something was missing, but the pressure of his intrusion had me reflexively tensing.

"Easy, baby. Try to relax. I don't want to hurt you more than I already have."

I nodded and took a calming breath.

"Thatta girl." His voice grew tight with strain. He rocked into me one slow inch at a time until he was buried all the way to my womb. "Fuck, this tight little pussy was made for me."

"*God*, Bishop. I feel so full." The words were nothing but wisps of air. All my energy was focused on reconciling this strange new feeling of absolute possession. Of being totally and completely enveloped by a man. He had captured all my senses—rendered me helpless but to absorb his taste, touch, and even smell. He was everywhere and everything, and I couldn't get enough.

Then he started to move.

Slow and steady at first, he gradually pumped faster and harder until nothing else existed but our intoxicating connection. No expectations or rules. No consequences or responsibilities. We were suspended in a magical moment consisting of pure carnal desire.

He pressed my knees farther back, curving my spine and allowing him even deeper. I clung to his body, urging him onward and pleading for more.

"Is this what you wanted, kitten?" he asked through heavy pants. "To have my cock buried balls deep inside you?"

"*Yes.*" My eyes rolled back as a shimmering brilliance teased and sizzled between my legs. Like my orgasm before but different. More. As though any release I'd ever had in the past was just a sample of what was possible. Of what I was about to experience.

"Fuck, I want to see my cum drip from your wet pussy."

To my surprise, it was Bishop's filthy words that nudged me ever closer to the cliff's edge. I hadn't known words alone could be so erotic, but every time he spoke, my insides melted.

"*Bishop!*"

"My girl likes it dirty, doesn't she?" He was like a freight train, relentlessly tunneling us both toward ecstasy. "That's it, baby. Squeeze my cock. *Jesus.*"

My lips parted in a silent cry as a cataclysmic orgasm overtook me. It swept me away and temporarily erased me from existence. I was nothing but tingling sensation. A river of molten pleasure.

Bishop's release erupted with a growl that reverberated from deep in his chest. He clenched me close for three slow but deliberate final thrusts, his body bowed around mine.

I basked in the afterglow.

I'd done what I'd set out to do, and everything about the moment was utter perfection, aside from our little hiccup. I felt certain Bishop would get over my deception. If he felt half as blissed out as I did, he could forgive a multitude of sins. What other choice did he have?

TWO

I DIDN'T EVEN REALIZE I'D FALLEN ASLEEP UNTIL MY phone rang hours later. It was seven thirty at night, and Conner was calling to find out why the hell I hadn't shown up for work. I mumbled an apology, then tossed the phone back on the nightstand, only to roll over and realize the bed was empty.

The fuck?

I peered around the dark room. The setting sun cast only a soft glow through the shades, but I saw no signs of Pippa. No note or discarded clothes. She could have been waiting for me in another room, but something told me she was gone. Motherfucker.

I'd rolled onto my back after the best sex of my life, my sated kitten draped over me, and passed out. The two hours of sleep I'd had the night before had caught up with me. Feeling Pippa's soft body pressed against mine was the last thing I remembered. Shit. Had she tried to wake me? How long had she lain there, wondering if I would wake up?

Talk about firsts. I didn't think I'd ever been walked out on. It was usually the other way around—me slipping out of some chick's apartment, hoping to skip the awkward morning-after talk. I should have been happy, then. Right? She'd saved me the trouble of sending her on her way. Except what we'd done hadn't been an ordinary screw. Hell, the words Pippa and ordinary didn't even belong in the same sentence.

Instead of relief, I felt this strange clawing sensation under my skin. Irritation. I didn't like that she was gone. What the hell was wrong with me?

I shoved off the bed and made a quick loop of my apartment. My instincts were right—no sign of her. I didn't like not knowing if she made it home safely even though it had been light out when she left. I decided that I should check on her and make sure she was okay, trying to convince myself it was her safety that concerned me rather than finding out the reason for her disappearance.

Or worse, you could just want to see her again.

Fuck, this was bad.

I stalked back to the bedroom and took a quick shower. I needed to clean up just as much as I needed to clear my head. I didn't need this kind of complication in my life. A fucking virgin.

Jesus Christ.

She'd given every indication that she was anything but innocent, yet I felt her body give way the second I pushed inside her. A body that was temptation incarnate —feminine curves and skin soft as a ripe peach. She was fucking incredible, and I was her first.

What was it about that fact that made me feel so damn barbaric? Like I needed to bang my chest and drag her back to my cave where no other man could even look at her.

When I'd first met her before Conner's wedding, I couldn't deny her appeal. Warm brown eyes, sandy-blond hair, and sun-kissed skin like she'd lived her whole life on the beach rather than in Manhattan. Then there were the hours we'd spent together on the day of the wedding. She was so full of energy and life. It was intoxicating just to be near her. Her addictive nature was the whole reason I ended up agreeing to take her back to my place when I knew it was a bad fucking idea. She was Italian. Her uncle was the goddamn Moretti family boss, and I had cut up her v-card like an expired driver's license—utterly worthless.

A surge of anger clenched my jaw so tight I was worried I'd crack a damn tooth.

I could be pissed all I wanted, but it changed nothing. That was one bridge that could never be crossed again. The only thing that would help at all was to at least reassure myself the damn woman had made it home alive.

I got dressed for work, then forced myself to call Conner back. My boss and longtime best friend wasn't going to like hearing I'd fucked his new wife's cousin.

Should have thought about that before you had her up against a wall, dickhead.

I shook my head as the phone rang.

"You finally get your lazy ass up?" Conner deadpanned in lieu of a greeting.

"Wouldn't have overslept if you hadn't left me with such a mess to clean up last night. You know how hard it is to get blood out of white grout?" I'd cleaned up the remains of a dead Albanian after Conner had gone on the warpath. I was glad he got the fucker, but the cleanup had been a bitch.

"That asshole was lucky I needed to get home. Should have drawn it out for days," he muttered.

I grunted in understanding. Those ruthless Albanian fuckers had been after us for weeks and had even killed Conner's uncle. I couldn't deny his right to be pissed. I just wished he'd let out his anger in a plastic-lined cell where I didn't have to spend all damn night drawing blood out of concrete.

"You call to argue with me or what?" Conner asked. His brevity didn't bother me. I'd known him since we were kids. I was closer to him than I was my own brother, which meant we gave each other shit regularly.

"You wish. I need Pippa's phone number."

Silence filled the air.

"Why?" The single-word response was filled with wariness.

I measured my words carefully, knowing my answer wouldn't go over well, no matter what words I used. "We didn't exactly make it to her parents' place."

"The *fuck?*" he roared.

I held the phone away from my ear and grimaced. "She's an adult, man. Practically begged to come back to my place."

"Doesn't mean you take her up on it. What the fuck have you done?"

If he only knew how bad it was, I'd probably need a surgeon after he got ahold of me.

"It's fine," I tried to assure him, "but I sort of passed out and need to make sure she got home safely."

"Jesus Christ, it just gets better."

"Yeah, yeah. If I'd wanted a lecture, I would have called my damn father. Just give me the fucking number."

Every silent second that ticked by was dripping with his disapproval.

"I'll text you," he bit out before the line went dead. Seconds later, my phone dinged with the number.

Taking a deep breath, I dialed Pippa and waited.

"Hello?" The sound of her sexy, vibrant voice eased the vise that had clamped tight around my chest the second I realized she had disappeared. That was, until I heard a man's voice in the background.

"Let's go back to the bedroom. I've got something special to show you."

Every muscle in my goddamn body threatened to snap with strain. Who the fuck was with her?

"It's me," I forced past clenched teeth.

"Oh!" she said with genuine surprise. "I didn't know you had my number."

"Am I interrupting something?" My voice was as sharp as a blade. It was a little much, but I couldn't help myself. The thought of her already off with someone else had me itching for a fight. "It's only been a few hours since it was my bedroom you were checking out. Seems awfully quick to do more exploring."

"Excuse me?" Her voice dropped to a hushed whisper. "Are you seriously upset with me?"

"Not crazy about you running out after everything that happened." I could hear how crazy my words sounded, but there was no stopping them. Emotion got the better of me.

Pippa sighed. "Listen, it's not a big deal, okay? I'm sorry that I misled you, but you don't have anything to worry about. I'm not expecting anything from you."

I didn't think she could have said anything that would have pissed me off more. Like she thought I'd be relieved to cut and run.

I took in a slow, deep breath to calm myself.

"You and I need to talk," I managed to say in a civil tone just as the man's voice in the background spoke again, rattling my newfound control. "Who the fuck is that?" I demanded.

"Not that it's any of your business, but it's my *real estate agent*. No need to get your panties in a wad. I'm looking for an apartment, and one unexpectedly came on the market. Now, I don't want to waste his time, so I need to go."

"I need his name," I demanded.

"What? Why?"

"Because you're alone with this guy, and I want to know where to look should anything happen to you."

Another sigh. "You're being ridiculous, but I don't want to argue. His name is Clint McAllister. Happy?"

"Hardly," I shot back dryly.

"Bye, Bishop," she sang before the line went dead.

♦

"This is Tom Pruitt. I'm a lending agent at First National. We're trying to close on the Central Park South property and have some big problems here. I've tried to call Clint McAllister, who is listed as the buyer's agent, but he's not answering his phone." I infused as much authoritarian urgency in my voice as possible. People are innately followers. Present yourself with sufficient confidence, and you can get people to do just about anything.

"Oh! I'm so sorry, sir. He's with a client at a property right now." The receptionist's voice was wrought with worry. As I'd planned, she had no desire to be pinned with the responsibility of a sale falling through.

"This twenty-million-dollar deal is in jeopardy of not closing if I can't get to him. Do you know the address where he's at? I could send someone to get him a message in person."

"Yes, of course. Let me get that for you." Not bothering to check my name or credentials, the woman read off an address located not five minutes from my place.

Perfect. I should be able to get there in time.

"Thanks for your help." I hung up and rushed from my apartment.

Ten minutes later, I was stationed in the lobby of a swanky apartment building when Pippa and her real estate agent stepped off the elevator. She'd changed her outfit into a baby-blue sheath dress that brought out the golden color of her skin. The look was striking but professional, and I hated that she might have wanted to look nice for the asshole at her side. Clint McAllister was close to my age, maybe a couple of years older. He was fit, reasonably attractive, and standing ten inches too close to my woman.

Your woman? Have you lost your goddamn mind?

I didn't know what the hell had come over me, but there seemed to be no stopping it.

"Pippa, dear. I'm so sorry I'm late." I swept her in for a quick kiss, keeping her hand in mine after my lips left hers.

The shock in her eyes was almost comical. She darted a look from me to Clint and back before collecting herself. "Um, no problem. I'm not sure this place was quite what I was looking for anyway." She turned to her companion. "Clint, this is Bishop. Bishop, my *real estate agent*, Clint." She accented the word as if to say, *I told you so.*

I didn't care in the slightest, too caught up in the way she'd assumed her role as my girlfriend without making a scene. I was certain I'd get an earful later, but for now, she was mine. An unsettling degree of satisfaction swelled in my chest.

"Good to meet you, Clint." I extended my hand, giving his an extra-tight shake. His lips thinned as his gaze cut to Pippa.

That's right, motherfucker. Hands off this one.

I turned back to Pippa and continued. "I really think we need to stick to the East Village for you. Murray Hill is great for young professionals, but I'd say it's a bit lifeless for you. A little farther south, you get easy access to better nightlife while still staying close to Midtown. Maybe we can run by and look at something in that area."

Pippa frowned. "Actually, I've been thinking the same."

I squeezed her hand. "Try not to look so disappointed."

"I have a listing over there you might like, and the place is empty," Clint chimed in. "Owners left the furniture for staging but have already moved. We could run over there now if you two have the time."

"We'd love to," I responded quickly before she had a chance.

She eyed me briefly. "I'll let my driver know."

The second we walked into the lobby of the renovated building in the East Village, I knew I was right. Pippa's face lit up like Times Square on New Year's Eve.

The small borough was rich with old-world culture but modernized in a trendy, artistic manner that attracted a younger crowd. Pippa was too full of life to be happy in a community comprised of overworked day traders and lukewarm accountants. This transitional neighborhood was much more her speed.

Clint's listing was located on the twelfth floor, which I liked. I'd always preferred even numbers to odd. No good reason, they just felt more well-rounded.

"Clint," Pippa chimed when we reached the apartment entrance. "Would you mind if Bishop and I look around in private for a few minutes?"

His eyes cut to me hesitantly. "Sure, you guys go on in. I have a call I need to make anyway." He retrieved a key from a lockbox to open the door and stepped aside.

The second the door was closed behind us, Pippa whirled around and jabbed a finger in my chest.

"What the hell are you doing here?" she hissed quietly.

"Telling you we need to talk."

She frowned. "How did you know where I was?"

"Does that really matter? I want to know why you snuck out earlier."

"I didn't *sneak*." She scoffed, lifting her chin. "I just had no reason to stay. It was time for me to get home anyway, and you were sound asleep. If that's all we needed to discuss, you can leave."

An amused, fiendish grin tugged at the corners of my mouth. "I don't think so, kitten. I'm not leaving you alone in a strange apartment with another man."

"What?" Her jaw slacked open with bemusement. "I can take care of myself."

I prowled forward, forcing her to take a retreating step back into the wall. Once she had no avenue for escape, I spun her around, restrained her hands behind her, and had my hand up her skirt in two seconds flat. She gasped but didn't struggle, too shocked to react.

I brought my lips to her ear, kissing her neck once before squeezing her wrists just shy of bruising.

"All it would take is a few minutes, and your life would never be the same," I said harshly, accenting my point by pressing her harder into the wall until she whimpered. I'd kill any bastard who hurt her, but she needed to understand the dangers. That type of crime could never be erased.

Pippa's entire body trembled. "It's not your place to worry about me, Bishop," she said softly, her words no longer bristling with a challenge.

"That's where you're wrong." I slowly brought my hand to her sex, gently cupping her warmth. "*This* is mine now, and I protect what's mine." The words were past my lips before I realized what I'd said. They'd come from somewhere deep inside me, and I felt their resounding truth down to my bones.

I was staking my claim to Pippa Revello, and if she thought she was shocked, she should have heard the voices screaming in my head. I was starting to think I'd gone fucking insane.

THREE

His? I couldn't believe this was happening. I figured Bishop would be delighted to know I wasn't going to cling to him with expectations. He'd probably had sex with a hundred different women in his life. Why the hell had he decided he wanted more from *me*?

Because I was a virgin? Surely, I wasn't the only virgin he'd ever had sex with. And if that wasn't it, what had driven him to go out of his way to find me? I'd been too stunned to confront him when I first stepped off the elevator and saw him standing there, all predatory grace and righteous fury. The lighthearted side of Bishop was disarming. The edgier, intense side of him was downright fascinating. It had taken me nearly a half hour to shake free of my bafflement and demand answers. Except his response had only left me more confused. The odd part was, I got the sense he was just as puzzled as I was.

We finished walking through the East Village apartment in a daze. I commented on the quality of the fixtures in the kitchen. Bishop noted the advanced security system already in place. We drifted from room to room, ignoring the giant pink elephant walking behind us.

This is mine now, and I protect what's mine.

I had no idea how to react. Clint joined us midway through the tour, so we continued with the ruse of coupledom. It felt too awkward to explain that we were sorting things out after a one-night stand. And I wasn't ready to treat Bishop like some kind of stalker. He was a tad overzealous, but I couldn't blame him. He'd been bamboozled. Maybe after a day or so, he'd settle down, and things would get back to normal. Maybe he'd see a girl at a club to distract himself and realize he'd overreacted.

I rubbed at a sudden ache radiating through my chest.

What the hell was that? Was I ... jealous?

I couldn't fathom what had come over me. All I knew was the image of Bishop with another woman did yucky things to my insides.

We'd both lost our goddamn minds. That was the best explanation I could come up with. And on top of it all, I couldn't be fully upset that he'd shown up because he'd been right about the East Village. It was perfect for me, and I adored the apartment Clint showed us. In fact, I wanted to make an offer. That meant I needed to suck it up and tell my parents I wanted to move out.

Suddenly, living with them forever didn't sound so unreasonable.

Come on, Pip. You can do this. You need to do this.

Ugh. I'd been dreading the conversation, though I knew it was inevitable. I loved my life. I had money and privilege and parents who loved me. Mafia life was a sweet gig if you didn't mind the constant surveillance, ever-present threats on your life, and a father who terrified and drove away everyone around you. Nothing about my life was average.

That wasn't necessarily a bad thing. I had all the luxuries in life a girl could ask for. Enough that I should have been happy. I shouldn't have battled a constant ache to see beyond the walls around my magical Mafia kingdom.

But Eve *should* have been content in Eden, yet she still sought out the forbidden fruit.

That was how I felt about experiencing life outside my bubble. Yearning clawed at my insides more urgently with each passing day, and that inner voice had cried out louder than ever with my cousin's wedding. Seeing how quickly her freedom had been snatched from her grasp terrified me. Two weeks. That was all the notice she'd been given before walking down the aisle to a man she hardly knew.

Hell. No.

Not me. Wasn't happening.

I wasn't getting stuck with a stranger, and even worse, never seizing the chance to sample what else was out there. No way. This girl was going to live life to the fullest. Now that Noemi was back and life had a pulse again, it was time to focus on me.

◊

"You were out and about longer than usual today," my father noted once I arrived home. "Your mother said you'd gone to see Noemi this morning?" He looked me up and down, a wordless statement that I was dressed much nicer than I would normally be just to hang out with my cousin.

"I was there earlier today, then I came home and changed." I took a deep breath and focused all my energy on projecting absolute confidence. "This afternoon, I was out with a real estate agent. I've been looking at apartments and have found one I'd like to buy."

There. It was out in the open. Come what may, I'd at least started the process.

Dad's face scrunched as though he'd just been force-fed a spoonful of vinegar. "You went house hunting before even discussing it with us?"

I couldn't stop my gaze from briefly dropping to my hands in contrition. "Well, I knew you might not be thrilled with the idea."

"So you thought it would be best to just go behind our backs?"

"No, Daddy. I mean. Yes, but I wasn't trying to be deceitful. I figured it would be better to know for sure if that's what I wanted so that I didn't upset you guys for nothing." Not entirely true, but things were going downhill quick. I couldn't afford to ruffle his feathers any more than necessary.

His already thin lips pursed further. "I'm not sure I understand why you're even doing this. You're only twenty, and it's not like you don't have plenty of freedom here. Why pay for a place when you have a perfectly good home here where I know you're safe? You can move out when you're married. Besides, Aria is seventeen now. She needs you to be a good example. We can't have her turning eighteen and thinking she can run off into the city on her own."

Frustration bunched in a tight knot between my shoulder blades. "Daddy, I have to learn how to be independent," I tried to explain.

"No, you don't. There's no reason you ever have to struggle on your own."

I stepped forward and clasped his hands, begging him to understand. "I might not have to, but I *want* to. It's important to me. I need to know I can stand on my own two feet. *Please*, Daddy."

He frowned, his conviction wavering. "I'll think about it," he finally grumbled and pulled me against his chest. "I'm not ready for this, Pip. I'm gonna try, but it's a dangerous world out there. Setting you free without a man around to protect you goes against every fiber of my being."

"I know, Daddy. That's why I haven't pushed before. And I'm sorry to make you worry, but this means the world to me. I want to find my place out there, and I don't believe I have to have a husband to do that."

He pulled back and peered down his nose at me with mock indignation. "You say that like finding a husband is a bad thing."

I chuckled and poked him in the ribs. "It's not necessarily a bad thing, but it's also not the *only* thing."

He studied me skeptically. "I suppose you're not entirely wrong."

I flashed him a brilliant grin, and he shook his head.

"Have you eaten?" he asked, moving on to safer waters. "You missed dinner, but I think there are leftovers in the fridge." At his mention of food, I suddenly realized that I hadn't eaten and was positively ravenous.

"Leftovers sound perfect. Thanks, Dad." I kissed his cheek, smiled warmly, and went in search of food with a renewed energy in my step.

♦

AN HOUR LATER, my stomach was no longer making angry noises, and I'd sprawled on my bed in my comfiest set of sweats.

What. A. Day.

I'd learned that my uncle had killed his wife and kept

my cousin under lock and key, lost my virginity, found a place to live, and admitted to my father that I wanted to move out. Talk about getting the ball rolling.

All in all, the day's successes easily outweighed the setbacks. I wasn't sure how to deal with Bishop, but there would be time to figure that out. I had to sort my feelings on the matter first. He wanted more from me, but that wasn't a part of my plan.

Would more necessarily be so bad?

Knowing how Mafia men worked, it just might be. Would he want to keep me under his thumb like my father tended to do? Dad was motivated by love, but I didn't want to be coddled anymore, no matter the reason. I wanted to make my own decisions and go where my heart led me. How was I supposed to do that with a man hovering at my side?

And on top of it all, Bishop was Irish. What did I even know about the Irish? Not much. I'd never given them much thought because the possibility of my involvement with them had been infinitesimal. Would my father flip out if he knew? Things weren't the same as when my grandparents were young, but that didn't mean my Mafia family would look kindly on me dating a member of a rival organization. At least with Noemi's marriage, we were now somewhat allied. In theory.

The lightness that had settled in my chest after talking to my dad thickened into a heavy mass. Normally, I found optimism second nature, but uncertainty was a shadow blocking my sunshine. It was hard to focus on the positives when my mind kept dwelling on questions surrounding Bishop.

As if summoned by my thoughts, a text from him appeared on my phone.

Bishop: I can still smell you on my sheets.

My grin couldn't get any bigger. I wasn't supposed to want his attention, but reminders of his dirty words thrummed in my veins and heated my blood. The memory of how he made me feel sprouted into a craving for more, insistent enough that I found myself typing a reply.

Me: I can still feel your hands on me.

I hit send, biting hard on my lower lip and praying my father didn't monitor my messages. I supposed if he did, he was in for a shock.

Bishop: You alone in your bedroom?

My heart did a full three sixty in my chest.

Me: Yes. Are you?

I had a feeling I knew where this was headed, and I also knew I shouldn't encourage him, but I'd never sexted before. If I wanted to try all the things, it would be counterproductive to pass up the opportunity, right?

I nearly jumped out of my skin when the phone rang.

"Hello?" I was too on edge to answer with anything sultry or sophisticated.

"Get on the bed." The commanding tone of his deep voice had my body moving without hesitation.

I clambered onto the bed and reclined on pillows propped against the headboard. Every nerve ending in my body sang out a chorus of anticipation.

"And what about you?" I asked, craving a mental picture of my own.

"I'm in my office now, and I'm already so fucking hard it hurts."

I smiled in satisfaction. "Sitting at your desk?"

"Mmm ... with you on my mind all goddamn day. I want you to slip your hand into your panties. Don't take them off, naughty kitten. This is a secret, just you, me, and that pretty pink pussy of yours."

Jesus, his words did unholy things to my insides.

When my fingers slid between my folds, I was already drenched. A small gasp slipped past my lips, drawing another groan from him.

"Fuck, no matter how hard I grip my cock, it's no comparison to the way your pussy milked me dry. You're a goddamn wet dream."

"Keep talking like that, and this won't last very long." I breathed shakily, half lost in my building pleasure.

He grunted. "You've touched yourself before, but what about this? Has another man ever controlled your body like this from a distance?" His voice took on a hard edge that made my heart rate tick up a notch.

"No, this is another first for me."

A masculine rumble of approval purred across the line. "Good. I want all your firsts, and there's so many to be had. Fuck, kitten, just thinking about it has me on the edge."

He wasn't alone. I was so swept away that the full breadth of his comment didn't register. My breaths grew shallower as my hand quickened its pace, and a crescendo of sensation built into a cataclysmic storm deep in my core.

"Don't you come yet. Not until I say," he ordered gruffly.

"But ... but I'm so close," I whimpered.

"Not until I say," he commanded.

"Oh *God*. Bishop."

"That's it, baby. Bury your finger deep inside and think about how much better it'll be when it's me filling you again." With his voice in my ear, it was impossible not to imagine him there with me. The feel of his body above me. The scent of his masculine cologne filling my lungs. The sting of his teeth over my sensitive nipple.

"*Bishop!*" I cried.

"What a good little kitten. Come for me, and let me hear how good I make you feel."

The most wanton, animalistic sound I'd ever made clawed its way from my throat as my orgasm ripped through me.

"Oh fuck *yes*." Bishop's exquisite cry filtered to my ears from where I'd dropped the phone next to me and given myself over to the ambrosia coursing through my veins. Nothing else existed outside my euphoria. But after countless seconds, Bishop's voice again drifted to my ears, gently tugging my body back to earth.

"Fuck, you're nearly as hot over the phone as you are in person."

God, I loved every word he said—like he had a direct line to my innermost desires.

But what about *all your firsts* and claiming that I was

his? Now that my brain could function without an onslaught of erotic pleasure blinding me, the voice of reason filtered back to the forefront of my thoughts.

Stupid buzzkill.

I would have preferred to stick my head in the sand, but that wasn't my personality. I was a head-on kind of girl, and this situation needed to be addressed.

"Bishop, we need to talk."

"Not sure there's much to discuss, kitten."

Hell, I even loved that he called me kitten. It was a silly endearment that I probably would have scoffed at had I heard it in a movie, but damn if it didn't sound like pure gold on his tongue.

"No?" I asked with a touch of amusement. "What about the fact that I may not want to be yours?"

Was it possible to hear someone grin through the phone? I could swear I heard his dimples mock me from a distance.

"Pretty sure it's a done deal, but if you want me to prove it to you, I will." His confidence knew no bounds.

"It's not a done deal, Bishop. We hardly know one another."

His response filled my ears like warm honey. "I know you better than any other man has ever known you."

"That's not … You know what I mean." Flustered, I stumbled over my words.

"Either way you look at it, the answer's the same," he said smugly. "Now, it's time for you to get some rest. Sweet dreams, kitten. I know mine will be positively feral." The line clicked dead, but I called his name several times, thinking surely, he hadn't just railroaded the conversation, then hung up. However, that was exactly what happened.

Bishop was every kind of stubborn yet somehow endearing at the same damn time. He had me so confused I didn't know if I wanted to scream or laugh. Maybe a little of both.

Not wanting to kill the last remnants of my orgasmic buzz, I decided to worry about Bishop later. He wasn't going anywhere, after all. He'd made that one point perfectly clear.

FOUR

"Line up for two-ball passing!" My brother's basketball coach's booming voice carried over the noisy gymnasium.

I'd been sitting on the old wooden bleachers watching Gabe's practice for the past half hour. Dad always made sure someone could stay whenever any of us had practices or club meetings. Now that I was older and not involved in extracurriculars, I'd become a monitor for my siblings. I didn't mind. Gabe was getting big so fast. At twelve, he was already my height. Not that I was particularly tall, but I remembered when he came home from the hospital, face puffy with the tiniest toes

I'd ever seen. With eight years between us, I was old enough to help raise him and took almost as much pride in his milestones as our parents.

I watched the boys amble into position for the drill, pulling out my phone when it buzzed with a text.

Bishop: How's Noemi doing?

It had been two days since I'd parted from Bishop. Two very eventful days, which had each ended with texts from him checking in. The day after he showed up at my apartment viewing, Noemi's father had been killed by her husband in order to save her life. I was so damn relieved my uncle was out of our lives, but the event was traumatic, and both Noemi and her brother were shaken.

Me: I think she's okay. I've only talked with her on the phone.

She and her husband had been holed up at their apartment. I didn't blame them. Witnessing a parent's murder, no matter how bad a parent, would be a horrifying experience. I'd thought about my cousin nonstop over those forty-eight hours—that and how undeniably sweet it was that Bishop had reached out each evening.

I was certain Bishop's Irish family had been just as busy handling damage control as my family had been. I'd hardly seen my father in two days.

Bishop: Were your families close?

Me: Our moms were twins, so yes. But we weren't close with her dad, if that's what you're wondering. He was never around much.

Bishop: Not even your father?

I wasn't sure what he was getting at. Was it just curiosity, or was he digging for information?

Me: Nope. My dad can be a bit much, but he's nothing like Fausto was. They weren't friends.

Me: That why you texted? To ask about my family?

I smirked as I sent the text. Goading him was so much more fun than it should have been.

Bishop: Careful, kitten. That sassy mouth of yours is going to get you spanked.

Jesus. My heart took a swan dive deep into my belly.

Me: That might be awkward in the middle of the YMCA. I hear they frown on spanking.

If I didn't get control of my idiotic grin, the people around me were going to think I was a nutcase.

Bishop: What the hell are you doing at the Y?

Me: Brother's basketball practice.

My eyes bounced between my brother and my phone for the next ten minutes as I waited for a reply. When I realized I was acting like a love-sick idiot, I quickly tossed my phone back into my purse.

What the hell was wrong with me? What voodoo magic did Bishop wield that he could undo me so easily? I didn't even want a relationship with the guy. Why did I care if he called or texted?

I heaved a frustrated sigh and dropped my chin into my hand, my elbow propped on a knee.

"It can't be *that* bad." Bishop's amused voice engulfed me as he lowered himself to sit on the bench beside me.

I shot upright. "What are you doing here?" My words

might have come off accusatory, but inside, I was bursting with exhilaration.

"I was heading to my gym, which happens to be nearby. Figured I'd pop in."

"But there are two dozen YMCAs in this city. How did you know which one I'd be at?"

"This is the one closest to your parents' house." He shrugged. "I could have been wrong, but I only would have been out a few minutes of my time."

I slowly relaxed, the adrenaline rush fading. "You have a habit of showing up places. Should I be worried?"

He flashed a fiendish grin. "Absolutely."

I shook my head, fighting back a smile.

"So who are we watching?"

"The one in the red shirt." I pointed out my brother on the court.

"You always come to his practices?"

"No. Mom usually takes him."

Bishop leaned back, draping his arms on the bench behind us. "Place brings back memories."

"You play?" I asked him.

"Every day when I was a kid. Not at this same Y, but they're all similar. We also had an outdoor court near my parents' house that I went to a bunch."

"You still play?"

"Not often," he said with a touch of remorse. "I'm usually boxing if I have time."

"If you love basketball, why pick up boxing?"

"Needed to know how to protect myself and fell in

love with the sport. There's no better stress reliever." His eyes cut over to me. "Well, maybe one."

The dizzying swell of electricity sparked between us. No matter that we were in a smelly gym surrounded by strangers, that damnable chemistry connecting us refused to dissipate.

I turned my now crimson cheeks back to the boys as they finished practice.

"Doesn't look like this court is scheduled for another practice," Bishop noted, peering around the sidelines. "I happen to be dressed for the occasion. Maybe I could show you a few moves."

Oh, this was too good—an opportunity I couldn't pass up.

"I'm not sure jeans and a T-shirt are gym clothes. Besides, I wouldn't want to keep you," I offered, not wanting to look too eager.

"Wouldn't want to be anywhere else." The cheeky bastard winked, and *God*, did I love it.

I texted our driver that Gabe and I were sticking around a bit longer, then descended the bleachers.

"Gabe, this is Bishop. Bishop, my brother, Gabriel."

"Gabe. Just Gabe," my brother corrected.

I smirked, knowing he hated to be called by his full name.

"Good to meet you, Gabe," Bishop said as the two shook hands. "I used to play and thought since I was already here that we could play a round of HORSE or something. We could show your sister how to shoot."

Gabe's gaze shot to mine. I quickly hushed him with rounded eyes.

"Yeah, that sounds great," Gabe said, smiling wide.

"Horse?" I asked. "Why on earth is a game involving basketball called *horse?*"

"That's just the word that's used. Whenever someone makes a basket, the others have to shoot from that same location. Whoever misses adds another letter in the word horse to their tally. The first to get all the letters and spell horse loses."

"Gotcha." I nodded sagely. "So where do we start?"

Bishop bounce-passed a ball to me. "You pick any spot you think might be an easy shot for you to make. If you don't make the basket, Gabe here will get to try a shot from wherever he chooses. However, if you *do* make the basket, then Gabe and I will try from that same spot. If one of us doesn't make our basket, that person gets the letter H."

"Sweet. Okay. Let's see." I propped the ball on my hip and wandered the court. First, I assessed a spot a few feet from beneath the basket before migrating a bit farther. And farther. Until I was just beyond the three-point line. I shrugged. "This looks good."

Bishop's brows rose to meet his brown curls. "You sure about that?"

"It's just for fun, right?" I bounced the ball a few times, sighted the basket, then lofted a textbook three-pointer. Nothing but net.

Bishop burst into a fit of laughter. "Oh hell, I've been

hustled like a chump. I'm surprised you didn't try to put money on the game."

"I don't need your money. Your pride will suit me just fine." I tossed the ball to Gabe, who was grinning ear to ear. "Your shot. Show him what you've got."

Our competitive natures drew out the game to a solid half-hour affair of heckling and gamesmanship. But in the end, I pulled out the win and relished every second of it.

"How long did you play?" Bishop asked as we collected our things.

"All through school."

"You should play pickup sometime."

I shrugged. "Maybe." The game was fun, but I was trying to get my parents to see me as an adult, and playing basketball didn't seem like it would help my cause.

Realizing Bishop planned to walk us outside, I paused at the entrance. "You should probably wait here. Our driver doesn't need to see that we had company."

"Is my being here a problem?" A shadow of concern darkened his features.

I didn't want him to worry, but I also wasn't ready to answer questions about him to my father. "Look, this was fun, but I told you that I wasn't looking for anything."

"Neither was I, but sometimes you end up in places you never meant to be."

Impossible brute. I wanted to slam my fists into his

chest and order him to leave me alone while simultaneously kissing him senseless.

Instead, I just shook my head, bewildered. "Good night, Bishop."

"Night, Pip." A slow, sultry grin crept across his face. "Sweet dreams." His words were a dark velvet caress that liquified my insides.

As if he knew exactly how he affected me, his eyes warmed to liquid molasses.

I was in so much damn trouble.

FIVE

"HEY, PIP. MIND IF I COME IN?" MY FATHER STOOD AT MY open bedroom door. It wasn't like him to seek me out. He was a busy guy and not the most hands-on type of father, so his unexpected appearance had me instantly curious.

"Of course, come on in." I'd been mindlessly scrolling on my phone, trying to ignore the fact that I hadn't heard from Bishop in two days. Or, more to the point, trying to ignore the fact that part of me was disappointed that I hadn't heard from Bishop in two days. I wasn't sure how a person could be so damn conflicted. If any more shots were fired among the voices in my head, I was going to find myself locked up in a cute little padded cell of my very own. "What's up?"

Dad sat on the edge of my bed, leveling me with a curious stare. "A young man came to visit me today. He said that you two have been seeing each other."

He didn't. He wouldn't.

I internally cringed.

Wouldn't he? Hadn't he made his position perfectly clear? Still, I was dumbfounded.

Dad plowed ahead, not registering my astonishment. "Why didn't you tell us you were seeing someone? And an Irishman, no less."

My lips parted, but nothing emerged. I had no clue what to say or how to explain.

Well, Dad. We had a one-night stand, so I didn't think it was worth mentioning.

Riiight. My father had never raised a hand against me in my life, but that just might do the trick.

"We've only seen each other a couple of times." I decided that was safe enough to admit.

"I'm not thrilled about him being Irish, but knowing you and Noemi, I shouldn't have been surprised. You two always were more like twins than cousins. With her married to one of them, I should have known you'd follow suit," he grumbled wearily.

"We are *not* getting married," I assured him.

"Well, I'm just letting you know I don't disapprove."

My brows drew tightly together as I studied my

father. "I don't understand. When I was in school, you did everything you could to keep me from dating. Now you're just suddenly okay with it?"

"It wasn't the dating that bothered me, per se. There was just no point in any of those boys sniffing around what they couldn't have. I wasn't about to let you get involved with some asswipe future accountant or insurance salesman who couldn't protect you. They don't have a clue about our way of life. Bishop can take care of you, even if he is fuckin' Irish." He said the last part almost under his breath.

I was a little stunned but not so distracted as to forget what started this little talk. "What exactly did you and Bishop talk about?"

"Not a lot, but he asked permission to formally pursue you, which I respect. Would have preferred hearing about this from you, however."

"I'm sorry." I conceded somewhat reluctantly. Technically, I held firm that it wasn't any of his damn business. "So what did you tell him?" If these two men had already started talking about weddings, someone was going to lose an eye, and it wasn't me.

Dad waited to answer until I'd brought my eyes back to his. "I said I had no objections, so long as it's what you want."

My gut did its best pretzel impersonation, twisting until I felt my stomach rise into my throat. I was so damn torn. I liked Bishop—a lot—but the whole point in screwing him was to experience life, not get myself tied down even faster. Getting hitched to the first man I slept with was exactly what I'd been trying to avoid.

My father stiffened when I didn't immediately answer. "All you need to do is say the word, and I'll make sure this guy never bothers you again."

"No!" I blurted. "It's not that, exactly. Everything is just happening fast. I'm confused is all." I didn't want Bishop to push me into a relationship, but I also didn't want my father to hurt him. My entire body recoiled at the notion.

"You don't have to do anything you're not comfortable with, Pip."

"I know, Daddy. Thank you."

He sighed heavily. "I suppose I should have talked to you before asking him to dinner."

"Dinner? Tonight?" Bishop was coming here to eat with my family?

Dad stood. "You're right. It's too quick. I'll give him a call and tell him we need to reschedule."

My hand shot out instinctively to clasp Dad's forearm. "No, that's okay. I was just surprised."

Seeing Bishop again after two days of silence was too tempting. The tease of his intoxicating presence was too alluring. I couldn't send him away.

"If you're sure, he'll be here in an hour." Dad studied my face as if searching for doubts.

I smiled softly. "Okay. Thanks, Dad." I was glad my father was on my side, even if he was overbearing at times. He always meant well.

Dad lightly tapped the faint cleft in my chin before leaving me to my dizzying thoughts.

Bishop had gone behind my back and spoken to my father. He'd disregarded my objections, then brought my *parents* into it without any consideration as to how that might make me feel.

The more I thought about it, the angrier I became.

The underhanded asshat had tried to force my hand by inserting himself into the equation. I liked the guy more than I should have, but he would have to learn I wasn't the object of a negotiation. I had thoughts and feelings and desires, and not one of them appreciated being disrespected. If he wanted to win me over, my opinion was the only one that mattered. Not my mom's. Not my dad's. Mine. And I would not be bullied into anything less.

Bishop needed to understand that I wasn't the pawn on his chessboard or even the king or queen. I was his opponent across the table. We both had equal stakes in the game, and cheating wouldn't be tolerated, which was exactly what he'd done when he'd gone behind my back.

I needed to send him a message that he'd messed up —show him that he wasn't the only one who could play dirty.

Thinking fast, I dialed an old friend from high school. Thanks to Dad and my love of basketball, that was all any of the guys from school were to me. I had been Queen of the Friend Zone. I'd hated it at the time, but it meant I had been accepted as one of the guys, and it was time to finally cash in on that unfortunate designation.

"Pipsqueak! Long time no see."

A beaming grin lit my face. "Hey, Archer. I need a favor."

SIX

Nonviolent might have been an odd characteristic for a boxer, but that was how I would have described myself. I wasn't quick to anger, and I certainly didn't have a lust for blood. I liked competition, physical exertion, and the strategy required to take on an opponent one-on-one. That was me in a nutshell, but the second I walked into the Revello dining room and laid eyes on Pippa seated next to another man, I saw red —blistering, boiling, crimson licking at the edges of my vision.

Gino Revello stilled beside me in the arched entry. "Pippa, I didn't realize we had another guest. Perhaps you should introduce us." Each word was laced with irritation almost imperceptible to the naked ear. Almost.

She smiled, unfazed, as though the sudden tension in the room had been her plan all along. What was her goal? Was she making a statement to her father or me? If I was her target, she had a thing or two to learn about the Bohanan iron will. I lived for a challenge, and Pippa's antics only spurred me on. If she was trying to deter me, she'd gone about it all wrong.

"I'm so sorry, Daddy. Archer was getting ready to head back to college, and this was the last night we could catch up. I hope you don't mind." She placed a hand on the asshole's shoulder, her words saccharine innocence.

I stepped forward and extended my hand toward Archer. "The more the merrier, I'd say. Name's Bishop." My smile was practically lupine, but I couldn't help myself. This was going to be fun.

"Mr. Revello, I hope I'm not intruding," he offered to Gino in a voice cracking from the pressure. This guy was no competition. In fact, the notion was laughable enough to help rein in my temper.

"Not at all," Gino assured him. "Guests are always welcome." He turned to me with a thin smile. "Please, have a seat." He motioned toward the empty place setting next to where his wife would presumably be sitting. The seat directly opposite Archer. Perfect.

I took my place and noted Pippa fiddling with her hair—a nervous tell. She'd put on a bold front so far, but uncertainty worried her insides. I had to admire her efforts. She was dedicated to paving her own path. Few people knew themselves with that sort of conviction and stayed true to themselves.

Reluctantly, I turned my attention from Pippa to her *friend*. "So, Archer, how do you know Pippa?"

"We hung out at school. We both played basketball, so we'd see each other at practices." His eyes cut briefly to Gino before he fidgeted in his seat.

Pippa took a sip of wine. "You would have met him before, Daddy, if you hadn't been so strict about me not dating."

Archer's eyebrows rose as he peered at her in surprise. He recovered quickly, but the damage had been done. These two hadn't been remotely intimate. Had he wanted a relationship? Why hadn't he pushed for it? Their situation was intriguing in a morbid, nauseating way. Had I not known Pippa was a virgin before she met me, the uncertainty of their past would have eaten me alive.

"Sorry for the delay." Mrs. Revello swept into the room carrying a steaming bowl of pasta in her hands. "Dinner is ready." She placed the dish on the table, followed by two teenage girls who did the same with the dishes they carried.

Gino stood. "Lauretta, this is Bishop Bohanan and ... Archer ... I'm sorry. I didn't get your last name."

"Worthington." He nodded to Lauretta. "It's a pleasure to meet you."

Pippa's mother looked from Archer to me and back

again. "Oh yes. It's lovely to meet you both. Uh, Ari, please go get your brother."

The older of the two girls left the room while the other took a seat next to Archer, allowing a curtain of hair to form a barrier between them. She appeared to be the shiest of the bunch.

"You have a beautiful home, Mrs. Revello," I offered.

She smiled warmly. "Why, thank you. Can I pour you a glass of wine?"

"Please, allow me." I stood and took the bottle from the middle of the table, giving her a healthy portion before pouring my own glass.

"Hey, Bishop!" Gabe's boisterous voice called at my back as he entered the room.

I set down the wine and stepped away from my chair, extending my hand for a fist bump. "What's up, man?"

Gabe beamed, clearly delighted to be treated like a peer. "Not much."

"Have you two met before?" Gino asked.

"Bishop came by practice the other day and got schooled by Pip." He grinned. "You should have seen her. It was great."

Archer chuckled, and I had to refrain from glaring at him.

"Yeah, well. Now that I know her penchant for *hustling*, I'll be more careful in the future." My gaze drifted to Pippa, an entirely different sort of hustle on my mind. Her thoughts must have taken her to the same place because a crimson flush warmed her cheeks.

She cleared her throat. "It's good to keep a few aces up your sleeve. You never know when someone will try to catch you off guard." Her comment was meant as a jab, but I was more amused than anything.

I raised my glass in the air, my eyes never leaving hers. "Words to live by, I'd say."

Archer fidgeted. Again.

Mrs. Revello sat taller. "Now that we're all here, please eat."

She motioned to the food, and we launched into the process of loading up our plates. The next hour was spent in polite conversation, often focused on Archer, thanks to my repeated efforts to keep the spotlight bearing down on him. Dinner didn't go quite as I'd expected, but it was still endlessly entertaining. By the time our dessert plates were licked clean, I suspected Archer would have paid money to be anywhere but in that dining room.

"Excuse me for a moment." Pippa stood. "I need to run to the restroom." She slipped away, my gaze trailing her.

Gino rose to his feet as well. "Why don't we head to the living room for an espresso or perhaps some Grappa."

"That sounds perfect. I need to make a quick phone call, then I'll be right there." I nodded in appreciation, then followed Pippa. My true intent was obvious, but I didn't care. In fact, I preferred everyone in the room knew exactly where I was going.

I waited for my naughty kitten outside the

bathroom, and the second she opened the door, I quietly forced my way inside.

"What the hell do you think you're doing?" she hissed once the door was closed behind me.

"I'm having a private word with you." I stepped closer. She inched back, her backside reaching the vanity.

"Well, good, because I have a thing or two to say to you. You can't just tell my father we're seeing each other and get yourself invited to dinner. That's not the way things work."

The invisible force field lassoing us together coaxed me closer.

"Nothing about this thing between us is normal, Pip. I've never in my life met a woman who ran from me like you do."

She crossed her arms over her chest and lifted her chin. "Well, get used to it because I'm not interested."

"Not interested in what? Me? Because your body disagrees." My eyes trailed down the column of her neck, over her fluttering pulse point, and slowly down the perfect swell of her breasts pressing up at the edge of her dress's scooped neckline. I didn't even have to touch her for a shiver to wrack her entire body.

A renewed spark of anger flared in my veins. I pushed forward, pressing my body into hers. "Why, Pip? Why the fuck are you fighting this?"

She unfolded her arms and stiffened for a fight before unexpectedly softening. "I told you that I don't want to be tied down," she said softly, her voice betraying her vulnerability.

I wanted to be gentle with her, but I hated the implication. "Tied down? As in *stuck* with one man? That implies you want to fuck other people, and I've already told you that you're mine."

"I'm *not* yours, Bishop." Her eyes pleaded with me, though she'd find no sympathy where I was concerned.

I leaned in and brought my cheek to hers, one hand on her waist and the other splayed flat on the counter behind her. "Did you know that the first person who discovers a star gets to name it anything they want?"

She was silent for a second before slowly turning her head side to side. "No, but I'm not a star, Bishop. You can't own me."

"No one owns the stars, baby. Everyone can admire them from a distance, but that one man whose eyes first sighted that brilliant speck of light and recognized it for the treasure that it is, that man will always have a special bond with that star." I trailed my hand up until the back of it grazed the underside of her breast.

Her back involuntarily arched, pressing her body further into mine. When her lips parted on a shaky inhale, I seized the opportunity. Our mouths came together like two halves of the same whole, perfectly shaped for one another. Savage joy filled my chest at the unabashed way she responded to my kiss. She didn't just relax into my hold. Pippa met my hunger with a ravenous need of her own.

When I finally pulled back for air, we were both at a loss for words.

"We should probably get back," she murmured.

I caressed my thumb over her cheek, wanting to memorize everything about the way she looked when soft and kiss drunk. Her lips were the littlest bit puffy, and her cheeks pink. No one in that room would have any doubt as to what we'd been up to. Just as I'd planned.

"I hope you don't think this means you're forgiven," she whispered with zero fight behind her words.

"I wouldn't dream of it." I smirked. "Now, come on. It's time to get back to the others."

A satisfied grin warmed my face all the way to the living area, where everyone was gathered for after-dinner drinks. When uncertainty slowed Pippa's steps, I placed a possessive hand at her lower back.

"Why don't you get your guest a drink." I held Archer's unblinking stare and winked.

"Um, oh. Yes. Sorry, Archer. Can I—"

Archer shot off the couch, face reddening. "Actually, I really need to get going." He turned to Mrs. Revello and thanked her for dinner. "And you, too, Mr. Revello. It's been great, but I gotta go."

I drew my brows together in feigned disappointment. "You sure? It's still early."

He shot a wounded look at Pippa, then nodded. "Yeah, I'm heading out of town tomorrow. Need to finish packing." He waved and made for the entry with his gaze downward. Pippa hurried after him, no doubt to apologize, but I wasn't worried. My work was done. And after that kiss, I felt much more charitable. I could only hope Pippa would start to come around.

Never in my life had I encountered a girl so hell-bent on getting away from me. Especially when her body responded to my every command. My kitten was a little feral, but I'd show her just how good it was to be owned. Belonging to a man could be its own kind of freedom—protection, adoration, support, and companionship. I'd be her damn everything if she'd let me.

♦

PIPPA RESPONDED to my texts the following week but only in the most cursory fashion. It was maddening in a way I'd never experienced before. I'd thought dinner might be the last of her resistance and had tried to give her room to get used to the idea of me being around. I got the sense it wasn't working.

"Shit, you're gonna break my damn hand." Callum took off the training pad he'd been wearing and shook out his hand. He was a longtime friend who spent almost as much time in the gym as I did. We took turns doing partner pad training, but this time my thoughts had me getting carried away.

"Sorry, man. Got a lot on my mind."

"The girl?" He smirked.

"Unfortunately." I grabbed my phone and confirmed that she still hadn't responded to my text from that morning. All damn day and nothing.

"Maybe she's just not that into you."

I shot him an arctic glare. "You're walking a thin fucking line."

Callum raised his hands in surrender. "I'm only saying maybe it's not meant to be. Right girl, wrong time or something like that."

"I think she doesn't even know what she's running from. Just a fear of what might be. That's the reason I'm not giving up because I know it's unfounded. I'm not planning to keep her barefoot and pregnant."

"You sure you're not chasing just because she's running?" he asked warily.

"I don't think so, but who the fuck knows." I wiped my face with one of the hand towels nearby. "I'm going to hit the shower and head home."

He lifted his fist, and I tapped it with mine. "Good luck, man. Can't say I envy you."

I grimaced as I walked away. Maybe I was beating my head against a wall, but I couldn't seem to stop. My gut told me to fight for her, and the damn thing had never proven me wrong. I'd never given up easily when I went after something I wanted, and this was no time to start. I would find a way to show Pippa I was exactly what she wanted—what she *needed*—and nothing would stop me, least of all my own self-doubt.

Two hours later, I was showered and pacing my living room. Pippa still hadn't texted me. Giving in, I dialed her number and resorted to a call. The phone rang six times before her voicemail picked up.

Goddammit.

It was nearly ten at night on a Friday. Could she really be that busy, or was she just ignoring me? I stretched my neck from one side to the other. I'd never been so damn tense as I'd been all week.

Or so I'd thought.

Seconds after I ended the failed call, Conner's number appeared on my screen.

"What's up?" I asked, concern sharpening my voice. I wasn't scheduled to work that night, so a call from Conner had me on edge. Had something gone down at the club? We ran a multimillion-dollar underground gambling ring through a front known as the Bastion Club. Our activities usually flew under the radar, but every now and then, things got dicey.

"Nothing," he grumbled. "Abso-fuckin'-lutely nothing."

My face twisted with confusion. "Nothing? What the fuck is up with you?" It wasn't like him to call for no reason.

Conner sighed loudly. "Noemi and Pippa wanted to go out tonight. I let them go to LAVO as long as they took Shae with them, but I'm not happy about it."

Pippa was out at fucking LAVO, one of the hottest clubs in Manhattan? Every muscle in my body strained to the point of snapping. "What the fuck are they doing there?"

"Hey, don't yell at me. It was your woman who pushed for a girls' night out."

My woman. That couldn't feel further from the

truth. I'd have better luck corralling smoke than I did Pippa Revello. Jesus.

That was it. No more fucking around. It was time for one last-ditch effort to win her over. To prove I could give her everything she needed. And if she didn't want everything I had to offer, I'd finally admit that it wouldn't work.

She wanted to experience the world. I'd fucking give it to her.

"Whatever. I've gotta go." I hung up on him. With no time to waste, I called Callum.

"Yeah?" he answered, loud music in the background.

"I need you to head to my place," I barked at him.

"What? I have plans tonight."

"Cancel them and get your ass to my place." I grabbed my keys, explaining what I needed from him as I marched to the elevator.

SEVEN

SOME PEOPLE TALK THROUGH SITUATIONS TO COPE, WHILE others turtle—crawl into their shells and process internally. I was a turtler. When circumstances overwhelmed me, I withdrew from friends and family in order to sort through my thoughts and feelings. Mom called it disappearing into my cave.

My conflicted emotions about Bishop had pushed me to a point of turtling. I spent a solid week lost in my head, trying to decide what to do and how I felt. I thought about what I wanted from life and what it would mean to have Bishop be a part of that journey. I could feel my heart finding ways to rationalize a relationship with him. The independent side of me felt betrayed—like I'd given in to societal pressures to latch onto a man—and being upset about my feelings only made things worse.

With each day that passed, however, I inched closer and closer to a decision. I couldn't deny that I wanted to give Bishop a chance. The part of me that had lobbied so hard for adventure and freedom felt defeated. To assure myself that I was still me and no man could take that away, I decided to drag Noemi clubbing with me. It was only the second time we'd ever managed to go to a club, and it was made possible because of a woman named Shae. She was a part of the Irish organization and some kind of badass fighter. Noemi's husband insisted we take her as protection, which was no problem for me because Shae was awesome. And with her along, I was able to tell my dad my plans rather than sneak behind his back like I'd had to do before. Once Dad knew that Conner trusted Shae enough to protect Noemi, he agreed to let me go without my own escort.

I wore a stretchy white dress that clung to my curves, stopping just below my ass. It made my tan look spectacular and gave me the confidence to hide the fact that inside I felt like a train veering off its tracks.

Be the energy you want to attract. I'd read that on Instagram, and it struck a chord. If I projected independence and confidence, I would attract those qualities into my orbit, or so said the internet. I was still undecided on the matter.

"You are my idol," I told Shae as we walked into the

restroom after a couple of drinks. "I wish I was just like you in every way."

She chuckled and raised a brow. "No one's perfect, and no one has a perfect life."

"Yeah, but you're hot as hell, you can fight, AND you're not attracted to men. I wish I didn't like men," I grumbled as I closed my bathroom stall door.

"Who said I'm not attracted to men?"

"Um ... I don't know. I thought you were into women?" I could have sworn Noemi had hinted at Shae batting for the other team, but now that I'd had a few drinks, I wondered if I'd been wrong.

"I'm attracted to men. I'm also attracted to women. I just decided years ago that men weren't worth the hassle."

"A-*men*!" My overzealous cheer echoed in the marble-lined bathroom, making me giggle.

"Right?" Shae agreed. "If all things are equal, women are definitely the better choice."

I nodded as I finished my business. "So have you ever dated a man?" I exited the stall and caught her eyes in the mirror as she did the same. I was so freaking curious about her. How she'd learned to fight. Why she wanted to work alongside the Irish men. What conditioner she used to get such a glossy shine to her hair. All the important questions.

"A couple, but they rarely hold my interest." She dropped her gaze to the sink as she washed her hands. "We'd better get back out. I wasn't supposed to leave Noemi on her own."

When we returned to our table, Noemi was right where we'd left her with a round of martinis waiting for us.

"Drink up," she called. "And let's hit the dance floor!"

We clinked glasses, and the alcohol seemed to filter straight into my bloodstream. We'd already had margaritas with dinner and tequila shots when we first arrived at the club. I grinned at the warm buzz heating my skin. "Let's do this!" It was definitely time to dance.

A half hour later, Noemi and I retreated to the table while Shae continued to dance. The woman was a powerhouse, not even breaking a sweat.

"This is exactly what I needed," I told my cousin, grateful she'd indulged my last-minute request to go out. "And Shae is really great. I'm glad Conner sent her along even though it was unnecessary." I wasn't crazy about men always thinking we needed chaperones. What really needed to happen was for men to learn to behave like fucking civilized human beings, then we wouldn't be at risk. Like that would ever happen. The only way to change the dynamic was to be a badass like Shae. I peered back at her again in the crowd.

"And with her here, we didn't even need our fake IDs," Noemi chimed in, raising her glass.

"Hell yeah!" I clinked my glass with hers, but just as I started to drink, my eyes collided with a murderous stare across the room. "You have got to be kidding me."

Bishop speared me through with indignant accusation. His black-on-black suit was almost as dark as the noxious aura surrounding him. He was a pressurized storm of righteous fury, and I'd never seen anything more beautiful in my life. The intensity of chiseled features and calculated power. He was an angry god come to earth with only one thing on his mind. Me.

Breathing suddenly felt impossible. Had he known I was here? Could this have been a coincidence? Somehow, I doubted it. Then how had this happened? Had he followed me? My heart thundered in my ears louder than the bass pulsing from the speakers.

Noemi's gaze followed mine. She quickly pushed for an explanation, but I didn't have the capacity. I needed to get away like a rabbit from the hungry fox.

Grabbing her hand, I led us onto the dance floor, where Shae was already grinding to a Lady Gaga remix that had spiked the energy in the room. Our small circle moving in motion with the rest of the crowd gave me the buffer I needed. I was one tiny minnow in a giant school, and together with the alcohol, it allowed me to pretend none of this was happening. The perfect distraction. Well, maybe not so perfect.

I could still feel Bishop's eyes on me even though it had to be impossible. I was too buried in the crowd. Yet there it was. The possessive touch of his stare. As if we were all alone and I was dancing just for him.

When Shae abandoned our circle and a solid body slid in behind me, I didn't protest. It wasn't Bishop. I knew that just as well as I knew that Bishop would be pissed when he saw me pressed against another man. Good. Let him feel a fraction of the helplessness I'd felt since he barreled into my world, stealing away my plans and making me feel things I didn't want to feel.

I rolled my hips and lifted my hands to rest behind me around the back of his neck. The man smelled all wrong, but his hand splayed on my middle held me confidently against him, and he moved like a dream. A hazy dream that abruptly burst when I was yanked from the dance floor by a tight grip shackling my wrist.

"Noemi, call your husband to come get you. We're leaving," Bishop barked at my cousin, who clambered next to me, captured in his other hand. He let out a sharp, short whistle that instantly had Shae's attention. He motioned to Noemi, silently instructing Shae to watch over her.

I never even got to say a word to my cousin before being dragged from the club. I didn't fight him because I didn't want to make more of a scene than he already had. Instead, I waited until we'd reached the sidewalk out front to yank free of his bruising grip.

"What are you doing here, Bishop?" I held my arms wide with disbelief, drawing more than one curious stare. "How did you know where I was?" A swell of emotions collided in my chest—relief at seeing him again after a week apart and bristling outrage at the possibility that he'd followed me.

Rather than rising to the challenge of my implied accusation, Bishop almost seemed to grow calmer, but not in a good way. Carefree Bishop was now lightyears away. The man before me, outfitted in an impeccably tailored dark suit with perfectly styled wavy hair, was brutally intense, and every ounce of that seething ferocity was aimed at me.

"I thought we talked about this, Pippa."

"About you owning me?" I shot back, alcohol inhibiting my self-preservation instincts.

"About *you*. And *me*. About who has a right to touch you." His baritone voice grated against my skin with hostile possession, yet every muscle in his body was clenched with practiced restraint. He was a master of self-control in a way I hadn't expected.

"I was having a girls' night out, Bishop. Not hooking up."

"What you were doing on that dance floor had nothing to do with a girls' night and everything to do with me. You were sending a message, and I received it loud and clear." He was right. I had lashed out in an admittedly passive-aggressive manner and was feeling more and more embarrassed about it by the second.

I opened my mouth to start a subtle retreat but didn't get the chance. A large man stepped partially in front of me, angling himself between Bishop and me.

"Hey, man. Sounds like the girl isn't interested," the man slurred. I stepped out from behind him, knowing this wouldn't help matters, and ended up with his arm draped around my shoulders. "Don't worry, sugar. I got you."

I nearly gagged at his whiskey-soaked breath. This was bad on so many levels. If my inner alarm bells hadn't sounded before, they certainly did now.

"That's okay," I tried to assure him. "He's a friend.

You can go." I tried to extract myself from his hold, but he pulled me in tighter.

"Nah, you shouldn't have to put up with that shit," the man slurred. "Come back inside, and I'll buy you a drink." He grinned down at me and turned us back toward the front door, his hand drifting down toward my ass.

"Take your fucking hands off her before you get yourself hurt." Bishop's warning sliced through the night air with lethal calm.

The man twisted back around, finally releasing me. "That some kind of threat? Because I'm not afraid of a skinny cunt like you." He had several inches on Bishop and at least fifty pounds. It wasn't muscle, but still enough of a size difference to send my heart clambering into my throat.

Before I could say a word to defuse the situation, Bishop's fists shot forward in two vicious strikes that sent the man lifeless to the ground. He never even had a chance.

I stared in shock as blood began to seep from the man's nose. Onlookers gasped and hollered, some cheering and others exclaiming in anger as they drew closer to check out the scene.

A strong hand clasped around mine. "Let's get the fuck out of here," Bishop growled, pulling me away from the growing crowd. I was too stunned to do anything but follow.

EIGHT

BISHOP LED ME TO HIS CAR WITH SWIFT, PURPOSEFUL strides. Anger wafted in the air behind him, making me reluctant to fuss at him for hauling me out of the club. He had no right to do what he'd done. Though, to be honest, I felt a little bad about avoiding him all week. I kept telling myself time apart would remind me how important my goals were, but all it brought was a sense of loss and emptiness.

When he finally slowed to a stop at the passenger door of his car, he seemed to calm himself in a way that set me on edge even more than his anger had. "I'm taking you to my place. Get in." He opened the door, his brown eyes devoid of their usual warmth.

"What's going on, Bishop? You're scaring me a little."

His chest expanded with a deep breath before he closed the distance between us, one hand weaving its way into my hair while his thumb trailed gently over my cheek. "There's nothing to be scared of, kitten," he said gruffly but gently. "My only intent is to give you what you want."

The words were sweet, so why did I detect a hint of sadness behind them?

Guilt tugged at my heart. I hadn't meant to hurt him by resisting his attention. The relationship had come on so fast that I needed time to process how I felt. And it wasn't like he'd made it easy with his domineering tendencies. Bishop was a city-toppling earthquake shaking my foundations when I only wanted a quick amusement park ride. At least, that was what I'd thought I wanted. After a week of thinking, I realized ground-shaking tremors could be just as invigorating, if not more so.

I nodded and allowed him to help me into the car. We both remained quiet on the short drive to his place. I wished I could see inside his mysterious head and hear his thoughts. Why was he still willing to put up with me after everything I'd done? How could he be so damn certain he wanted me or that we'd be good together? Maybe it was age. He was several years older than me. Late twenties, if I had to guess. He'd likely had dozens of relationships in that time, hundreds if I counted his flings.

Ugh. Why had I gone there?

My stomach was starting to feel the alcohol, and the last thing it wanted was to picture Bishop with a host of other women. Making them laugh. Protecting them. Pressing them against a wall and ...

What are you, a masochist?

I cleared my mind as best I could and spent the rest of the ride watching the city lights out the passenger window. The conversation looming over us would be emotional enough; I didn't need to wind myself up unnecessarily.

Fifteen long, awkward minutes later, we were back at his apartment with a dense forest of unspoken words between us. Only, the conversation I'd thought we were about to have wouldn't be possible because we weren't alone.

A man Bishop's age stood in the living room, a whiskey in hand. He didn't seem surprised to see us, though he gave the impression of a man who didn't rattle easily. He was handsome in a rugged way. Strawberry-blond hair with green eyes and a swath of freckles made harder with a square-cut jaw and facial features so masculine he could have walked off the set of a *Vikings* episode. And he stared at me with an intensity I didn't quite understand.

"What's going on?" I blurted, all manners forgotten. I had thought we were going to talk about our relationship and finally come to an understanding, but the presence of another man completely threw me.

Something was horribly off, but I had no idea what.

"I'm giving you what you want," he said in a cool voice.

A wave of confusion washed over me, my eyes cutting to the other man. "What do you mean?"

"You want to experience life without limitations. I'm here to give that to you."

I looked from one man to the other, totally baffled.

"Pippa, I'd like you to meet Callum." Bishop extended a hand toward the stranger.

The man set down his glass and crossed the room to place a kiss on the back of my hand. "It's a pleasure to meet you," he murmured.

The gesture was so intimate, so unexpected, it set my stomach to spin cycle.

I turned to Bishop, leaving Callum at my back. "Is this...? Are you suggesting a threesome?"

My spine stiffened as Callum brushed the hair off my shoulder and pressed his lips to my neck. "This is whatever you want it to be."

Holy shit, is this real?

Two men? At the same time? I'd never even contemplated that in my daydreams. I'd been trying to achieve normal, never even imagining something so adventurous. A threesome would definitely be different and new. Was that what I wanted? A swarm of emotions clouded my head, preventing me from determining just how I felt.

My gaze sought out Bishop's for direction. Was this what *he* wanted? Considering the way he was acting, I didn't get the impression he was excited about the prospect.

"Why are you doing this?"

A hint of emotion returned to Bishop's eyes in the form of angry sparks. "Why?" he asked, closing in with Callum at my back. "I told you already. I'm giving you what you want. You want to see what it's like to be with other men. To keep your options open. This is the perfect opportunity."

Callum's hands cupped my waist. My heart hammered so fast that I couldn't catch my breath.

Bishop continued, his words growing more passionate. "You've told me you don't want to be tied down. That you want to sample what's out there. This is me showing you that if that's what you *really* want, I can give that to you. *For* you."

Was he offering some sort of open relationship? I was stunned. My brain couldn't keep up.

Bishop raised my hands over my head. "Maybe you want one of us to watch. Maybe you'd like both of us at once. That would be a new experience, wouldn't it, kitten?"

Callum trailed his hands down my sides, his hard length now pressing into my backside.

Was this really happening? Would Bishop share me if that was what I wanted? I'd read stories about that sort of thing, and it had always sounded hot, but the reality was a far cry from my fantasies. Maybe it was the glacial severity in Bishop's normally warm gaze, or maybe the fact that I didn't know Callum at all, but every muscle in my body was tense with apprehension.

This didn't feel good. Not at all.

"I don't think I like this," I stammered, tugging at my hands to free them.

Bishop held firm. "You don't have to resist, Pippa. This can be anything you want it to be," he urged.

Tears burned the back of my throat. I couldn't stand the torment any longer and twisted harshly away from them both. "Stop it! Just fucking *stop!*"

"Why?" he demanded. "Isn't this exactly what you wanted?"

"I never asked for any of this."

"Then how am I supposed to take it when you push me away and grind on other men at a club? You told me specifically you didn't want to be *tied down*. All I'm fucking asking is that if you need to explore, you do it *with* me. Is that so goddamn much to ask?"

Bishop had ripped open his chest and put his heart on display but done it in a hurtful, callous manner that wounded me deeply. He made me sound like the most heartless, shallow woman on earth. And maybe I was. It would explain the gaping chasm that hollowed out my chest, making me feel utterly empty.

We both turned to see Callum silently retreat from the room. The small break acted as a valve releasing a fraction of the pressure filling the air around us.

"I'm sorry," I whispered, eyes unable to meet his as they filled with tears. "I truly didn't mean to upset you tonight. It was actually the other way around. I thought about us all week. What I wanted and needed, and the difference between those two. I could sense where I was headed. That I was going to commit to giving us a try and stop pushing you away. It felt like I was handing over my independence, so I decided to go out. Like a retirement party. One last hurrah. When I saw you there, I just sort of panicked."

I finally lifted my gaze, showing him my hurt. The unexpected pain of feeling like an object to be passed around. He made out his actions to sound like a generous offering when, in reality, it felt like a defensive blow to lash out when he hadn't understood my reluctance to jump into a relationship.

"Fuck, this isn't how this was supposed to go." He coaxed my face to his, but I closed my eyes to shut him out. It was more than I could take.

I hadn't wanted Bishop to know just how deeply he'd upset me, but a treacherous breath hitched in my throat. His body stiffened the instant he felt my spasm.

"Please, don't cry." Bishop cupped my face in his rough hands and brought our foreheads together. We stood like that for endless seconds before he brought his lips to my forehead in a poignant kiss.

"I want to go home now." I forced the words past the python of emotion strangling my throat.

"Fuck, baby. I'm so sorry. I was only trying to make you understand how much I want you."

I nodded, ready to say anything to get away. I needed to be alone.

By some mercy of God, Bishop took my hand without further argument. I'd half expected him to keep me captive and demand to talk it out, but instead, he wiped my tears and led me to the door. Within minutes of returning home, I was back in my childhood bed and more lost than I'd ever been in my life.

NINE

For the first time since meeting Bishop, he'd gone completely silent. A solid week with no texts. No calls. No unexpected appearances. I felt as though the world had succumbed to winter months early, leaching the city of color and warmth.

How could that be? How could I feel so bereft when I'd known him for such a short time? When I'd only just allowed myself to admit my feelings for him?

One particular question haunted me day and night. Was this thing between us over?

I wasn't sure we had built enough of a foundation to

come back from such devastation. I couldn't help but wonder if it was all my fault. Had I rejected him one too many times? I had been so insistent that I wanted to be free of him, but now that sounded like the worst possible outcome. The thought of never feeling the searing heat of his ravenous stare brought on a head-to-toe shudder.

You could always reach out to him, you know.

There she was again. The voice of reason. She'd been goading me for days, but I couldn't seem to summon the confidence to make that first move. Did he hate me for being insensitive? Could he really care for me if he'd been willing to share me? All my doubts were quicksand, keeping me mired down in uncertainty.

I passed each day in a hazy melancholy, hiding in my room. The following Saturday, however, was to be spent almost entirely at a family wedding—a blessing and a curse. The Lucciano crime family, the most secretive and solitary of the Five Families, was hosting a massive gathering to celebrate the wedding of Alessia Genovese, one of the boss's daughters. The intrigue surrounding their family and rarity of such a unified event was a welcome distraction. But at the same time, a day spent gushing over love and forevers felt like the worst kind of torture because a niggling splinter of truth wedged its way further under my skin every day, screaming at me that I was allowing my chance at true happiness to slip between my fingers.

I'd wanted my independence, but at what expense?

What if I had, as my mother used to say, cut off my nose to spite my face? Did exploring all that life had to offer necessarily preclude me from a relationship? Wasn't that, in fact, one of the many facets of life I was looking to sample?

Deep in my gut, I knew the answer.

Seeing the bride and groom so happy together brought tears to my eyes. I was thrilled for them and upset with myself. I tried to convince myself that even if I couldn't fix things with Bishop, I'd learned a valuable lesson. That either way, I was better off. But when the dancing began, and a handsome young man asked me to dance, I didn't feel better off at all. I felt awkward and icky. I should have been flattered to have been approached. The guy was cute, and he knew how to move, yet all I wanted to do was cry because it wasn't his arms I wanted around me.

Sensing the sting of tears in the back of my throat, I apologized in a rush, then fled for the ballroom exit. My departure didn't go unnoticed. A minute later, the oldest of my two little sisters joined me on a bench in the grand hotel hallway.

"Want to talk about it?" Aria asked, bumping my shoulder.

"Not sure it'll do any good."

"I'm assuming this is about that gorgeous hunk of a man who came to the house?" she asked with a hint of teasing.

"Yup."

"He hurt you? 'Cause ... I know a guy."

Her joke was so unexpected that I coughed out a laugh that edged on a sob. "Not necessary, but thanks. And besides, I'm just as guilty as he is. We've both made such a mess of things."

"It may be trite, but dude, there are so many fish in the sea. Have you looked on Tinder lately?"

I gaped at her. "Ari! You have a Tinder account? You're only seventeen!" Dad would have an aneurysm if he found out.

"It's just a profile," she tried to assure me. "I don't have to interact with anyone if I don't want to. Aren't you even a little bit curious about what's out there?" She pulled out her phone and opened the app.

I was stunned my little sister had been so adventurous and a tiny bit fascinated with the images of the men who came up. We laughed at a few, and several might have piqued my interest had I seen them weeks earlier, but that wasn't the case now. None of them were what I wanted. None of them were Bishop.

"Come on, let's start a profile for you. It's super easy. I can even do it for you."

"No. I'm not interested, but thanks." I smiled. It was sweet of her to try to help. I only wished it were that easy.

Aria shrugged and stood. "I suppose that leaves us no choice then."

"Oh yeah?" I asked warily.

"Yup. The only thing left to do … is dance. Come on." She clasped my hands and pulled me back toward the enormous ballroom where Bruno Mars had everyone grooving to "Uptown Funk."

I wasn't as close to my sisters as I was to Noemi, but they were still my sisters, and they knew how to cheer me up. After the chicken dance and a boisterous rendition of "We are Family," I felt a touch more like my optimistic self.

TEN

"YOU EVER GONNA GET OFF THAT PHONE AND GET BACK IN the ring with me?" I barked at Callum. "I thought you were just taking a breather."

"Are you kidding?" He stared up at me incredulously. "Not when you're wound up the way you are. I'll lose a fuckin' kidney. You still haven't sorted things out with Pippa?"

A snarl teased at my upper lip as I rested my forearms on the top rope and dropped my gaze to the floor. "Just trying to practice some fucking self-restraint," I grumbled. "You really done for the day?"

I could have spent the entire day in the ring and not

fully extinguished all my pent-up frustration. A week away from Pippa hadn't been easy. She needed to think, and so did I. Not whether I wanted her—that was etched in my DNA for some godforsaken reason. What I had to figure out was how to get her to see me. To apologize and make her understand what we could have together.

"Yeah, man. I'm gonna find some entertainment for the night, then head home." His thumb swiped almost rhythmically on his phone's screen, only occasionally pausing. "Hold up." His eyes narrowed as he studied something. "I'll be damned." He held up the device, displaying an image of Pippa.

My blood ran cold.

"Is that fucking *Tinder*?" I barked, losing all vestiges of control.

"Yeah, man," he said warily. "But there's no telling when the profile was created or if she's even active."

I began to pace in the ring. He was right, but it didn't seem to make me feel any better. Had Pippa been on the app before we'd met? If she had, would she have still been a virgin? I couldn't say for sure, but I knew it didn't sit well. I hated the mere idea of her face out there for guys to creep on.

I'd been trying so hard to give her space, but I couldn't do it. That wasn't who I was. Pretending to be anything else would be pointless. I had to lay all my cards on the table and make this right. I'd fucked up, and if I didn't find a way to fix it, I'd lose her forever.

ELEVEN

REASON 342 TO LIVE ON MY OWN: NO REQUIREMENT TO attend Sunday evening Mass. I was *not* feeling it, but Mom and Dad insisted I attend if I didn't have other plans, so I forced myself to get ready for church. The last thing I wanted to do was talk to people. Normally, smiles came easily to me. Any semblance of happiness today would be pure show.

Sighing deeply, I turned off the light in my room and headed to the top of the stairs when the front door chimed. I stilled just out of view of the entry, hoping someone else would deal with whoever had stopped by.

Sure enough, Dad's commanding stride clacked on the wood floors before the door swept open.

"Bishop, I don't believe we were expecting you." Dad's stilted words filtered up, sending my heart rate into a frenzied pace.

Bishop was here? A part of me had been praying he'd reach out, while the rest of me was overcome with embarrassment at the prospect. It was safe to assume he was there for me, but why? To tell me how much I'd hurt him? To ask for a do-over?

If he wanted nothing to do with me, showing up at my house would have been counterproductive. That nugget of truth helped quiet the riotous doubts screaming in my head.

"I'm sorry to show up unannounced, sir. I really need to speak with Pippa."

"I'm not so sure that's a good idea," my father replied coolly. "She hasn't been herself for a week now. And if I was a betting man, I'd say you had something to do with that."

"You're right. I did something stupid, and even though I didn't intend to hurt her, I need to apologize. Please, let me do that." Bishop's voice was distant. I found myself straining forward to keep from missing a single word.

He was here, and he wanted to apologize! A flutter of cautious optimism filled my chest. I stepped forward and started down the stairs.

"Dad, it's okay," I called down to him. "I need to talk to Bishop."

My father turned to study me, his eyes narrowed. "I'm not sure that's a good idea."

The same time my foot reached the ground floor, my mother joined us in the entry. "I'm not sure that's your call to make. Let them sort out their business, Gino," she chided softly. "We were just about to head to evening Mass. They can talk while we're gone." She placed her hand in the crook of his elbow and called upstairs for my brother and sisters.

Dad scowled but didn't argue. My siblings thundered down the stairs, following my parents to the garage. Then Bishop and I were alone.

Was my house always that silent?

The absence of sound seemed to scream at me from all directions, urging me to say something. To propel us off the knife's edge toward a resolution, one way or another.

"I'm glad you're here." My words echoed in my ears, seeming so much louder than they'd been. I ignored the swell of awkwardness threatening to drown me and forged ahead. "When I first asked you to take me home with you, I was looking to assert my independence and experience life. Never in a million years had I considered it might lead to something more. What were the chances?" I peered up at him, imploring him to understand. "I never meant to hurt you. I was just scared. Everything you wanted was the opposite of what I'd told myself for years that I needed. You showing up at dinner and the nightclub? That freaked me out. I hope you can understand that."

He moved closer, taking my face in his hands. "This is my fault, Pip. I know that I've come on too strong, and that's not normally like me. You somehow make me do crazy things I never would have done before. Feel crazy shit I never would have felt before." He paused, his earnest stare piercing me through. "All I wanted was for you to give me a chance. You can still experience the world with me—anything out there, I'll give it to you. All you have to do is ask," he said fervently.

"I think I can do that," I whispered.

Instead of the warmth I'd expected at my answer, Bishop's gaze dropped, and his brows drew together. "I should have come talk to you sooner, and I'm embarrassed to admit that something in particular brought me here." His eyes returned to mine as his jaw clenched tightly shut. "I was with Callum earlier, and he happened to find you on Tinder. Please, tell me you didn't get on that damn app because of me this week."

"What?" I gasped, eyes wide. I couldn't fathom what he was talking about until my conversation with Aria came rushing back to me. My eyes drifted shut. "Aria," I groaned. "We were at a family wedding yesterday. A man asked me to dance, and I accepted because I felt like I should, but everything about it felt wrong. It was so disorienting and upsetting that I stopped mid-dance and ran. My sister found me in the hallway. I explained a little about what had happened between us. She insisted I needed to get out there. That meeting someone new would cheer me up. She told me to create a Tinder profile, and I refused. She must have created it behind my back last night because I've never even downloaded the app. Please, believe me. I had nothing to do with that."

A ragged curse tore from his lips as he swept me into a crushing hug. "Thank Christ." Relief gave his words wings, and they lifted me straight off the ground. "I hate the thought of you being with anyone else, kitten."

I held him tight for a second longer, then pulled back to meet his gaze again. "Then why did you set up that meeting with Callum?" I asked, a painful twinge searing through my chest. "Would you really have shared me?"

"I would have tried if that's what you truly wanted, but I would have hated every goddamn second."

"Then why did you offer?"

"Because that was the only way I could think of to prove that I'm not the prison sentence you seemed to think I was."

I shook my head. "No, it wasn't that."

"Then what?" His head tilted, eyes pleading for understanding. "Why have you been so resistant?"

"Because I've daydreamed for years about being *normal*. Life was supposed to be different for me— dating, travel, maybe even a job. I was going to be a normal girl and not get married off by my father to some man I hardly knew. Go from living under one man's roof to another's, never learning to stand on my own."

His lips quirked upward in the corners. "And who told you I would take that dream from you?"

I shrugged meekly. "Me. I've never known a Mafia

man who didn't keep his wife or girlfriend tucked away for safekeeping."

His eyes sparked to life with a flash of his beautiful dimples. "Lucky for you, I'm Irish, and we're used to our women being entirely too batshit crazy to control."

I choked on a laugh as a swarm of bubbling emotions summoned a new pool of tears.

Bishop placed a tender kiss at the corner of each of my eyes. "I'm not asking for forever yet, just that you'll give me a chance. Give *us* a chance."

I leaned forward hesitantly and allowed my lips to ghost against his. "I don't want to push you away anymore. I don't want it to be over."

"Whatever this is, kitten, it's not the end. This is only the beginning."

TWELVE

Bishop spent the next hour with me on the couch, watching a movie and talking. We cuddled and teased and laughed until my heart felt full to bursting. By the time my family returned, I had to rein in my obnoxious smile so that my dad didn't suspect something more had gone on while he was out.

I was reluctant to let Bishop leave when the time came but pleased when he asked me, with Dad present, if he could pick me up for breakfast the following morning. Dad looked at me as if to verify that I wanted to go and took my giddy grin as answer enough. I was so excited I could hardly sleep that night. It was amazing how freeing it was to allow yourself to feel what came naturally. I'd felt like I shouldn't want to be in a relationship, adding guilt and frustration to an already uncertain situation. When I simply allowed myself to enjoy the way I felt around Bishop, warm light seemed to flow through my veins.

That electric rush gave me the energy I needed the next morning when Bishop showed up bright and early after thoughts of him had kept me awake late into the night.

"Morning, gorgeous." His voice was raspy and sexy as hell. He took my hand in his and walked me to his car. "You sleep well?"

"I had a little trouble getting to sleep, actually."

"Oh yeah?"

"Yup. All kinds of happy, tingly thoughts kept me awake," I teased.

Bishop groaned from deep in his chest. "The things you do to me should be illegal."

"That's funny. I've thought the same about you—or, more precisely, your dimples."

He grinned at me. "You like the dimples?"

"Please." I scoffed, tilting my head to the side. "As if you don't know how damn sexy those things are."

"Still good to hear you say it." He pulled me close and kissed my temple before helping me into his yellow Mustang.

We rode in comfortable silence for a few minutes before I decided to ask a question that had danced in my mind for days. "Bishop?"

"Mmm?"

"Why me?" I asked softly, peering at him from the corner of my eye.

His gaze swept my way with amusement. "Why not you?"

"Because we hardly know each other. How could you have been so convinced you wanted me in such a short amount of time?"

"I don't have to eat two tubs of mint chip ice cream to know it's my favorite."

"Yeah, but people aren't ice cream," I chided playfully. My insides warmed at his molten gaze.

"No, but you taste just as sweet."

Hell, what had I been thinking to push him away? He was everything a sane, rational girl could want in a guy. And I'd been too stubborn to open my eyes and see.

"Where are we going for breakfast." A wash of embarrassment had me changing the subject.

"Café Bohanan. I hear the chef there makes a mean French toast." He winked.

A rush of pleasure swelled in my core. "Are you just taking me home to get me naked?" My voice grew as sultry as a summer night.

"No, but I'll admit that I can't wait for you to get your own place. I'd prefer easier access to you."

I studied him, taking in the way his thick lashes curled at the tips. "You really are okay with me getting a place, even if we're together?"

He smirked and accelerated onto the freeway. "Baby,

you can own half of New York for all I care so long as I'm the one in your bed at night."

If I smiled any wider, I was at risk of permanent damage. "You always know exactly what to say, don't you?"

His eyes softened as his gaze trailed over my face. "I say plenty of shit that pisses people off. That's why I'm so good at apologizing. Lots of practice." He sobered, his eyes returning to the road. "And I'm so sorry I hurt you last week. I can't promise to never do it again, but I'll promise to try."

"Okay," I breathed.

The thing about Bishop was he didn't hold back. He was exactly who he claimed to be. Said what he felt and spoke up when he had something worth saying. When he told me how much my happiness meant to him, I believed him.

It was amazing how much that knowledge turned me on.

I didn't make it five seconds after entering his apartment before I launched myself at him. Bishop lifted me easily into his arms, my legs wrapping around his middle.

"I was so damn worried I'd never have this again," Bishop said as he walked us back to the bedroom.

"Me, too," I admitted, kissing his jaw. The scrape of his scruff on my lips sent a zing of pleasure straight to my core.

He set me down next to his bed and stripped us

naked as if our clothes had been on fire. Then his eyes devoured me.

"On the bed, on your back. I need to taste that sweet cunt again."

Who was I to argue? I lay back, his hungry stare giving me the confidence to arch and twist provocatively. He wanted a show? I'd give him one.

"I could watch you move like that all goddamn day." He prowled closer and spread my legs wide as he kneaded my inner thighs with his strong hands. Hands that soon found their way to my aching breasts. I nearly came when his adept fingers pinched my nipples harder than I'd expected. Bishop wasn't being gentle. He was on a mission, and I was his to command.

He nipped and stroked, then soothed and teased until my body wept with the need to come.

"*Please*, Bishop. I need to come." My words were wrought with desperation.

Bishop aligned his body with mine, our hearts beating in tandem before he paused. "Condom."

I shook my head. "I'm on birth control."

"You sure? I don't want you doing anything you're not comfortable with."

"I don't want anything between us. No condoms or secrets or anything else. Just you and me," I said softly.

"Fuck, I don't know what I did to deserve you," he growled before his lips devoured mine. In three commanding strokes, Bishop was fully sheathed inside me. "*Jesus*, you feel incredible."

The fit was still tight, but my body was growing

more accustomed to accommodating his size. A throaty moan left my lips. Bishop took his time with long, intentional strokes. He sucked on my breasts and kissed my neck as a storm brewed inside me. Then, without warning, he pulled out and sat back on his knees. I didn't have time to ask what he was doing when he lifted my legs and flipped me onto my belly.

Bringing his body over mine, he purred close to my ear. "Ready for something new?"

I bit down on my giddy grin and nodded. His chest reverberated with a masculine rumble before he snaked an arm under my hips and guided my ass into the air.

"Arch that lower back." He pressed his wide palm on my upper back and lifted my ass with the other. The position felt so wanton and exposed, like a cat in heat presenting herself for the taking. It was fucking incredible. Not just the eroticism of the act but the way it made me feel to know Bishop's ravenous stare was devouring every tasty morsel.

"We are going to have so much fun exploring together." His hand caressed the globe of my ass before disappearing, then swiftly returning with a smack.

I gasped in surprise, then pressed my ass out farther as the warm aftermath of his spanking heated my core. I almost purred when the head of his cock nudged my entrance.

"Keep that ass tilted upward, baby. You got me too worked up for anything but hard and fast." He wasn't lying. The man fucked like an animal, and I loved every unholy second of it. The weight of his body on mine.

The slamming of his balls on my clit. I even liked how he gently wrapped a hand around my throat, careful not to inhibit my breathing. All of it felt divine, especially knowing I was his. This powerful, breathtaking, incredible man had chosen me, and he was all mine.

♦

"I SUPPOSE WE SHOULD GET COOKING," I said when we were still in bed a half hour later.

Bishop grunted. "Not sure I need food when I've got you to eat."

My stomach bellowed an angry growl in protest, and I burst out laughing.

Bishop raised a single dark brow. "My mistake. Come on, let's get my girl some breakfast."

A half hour later, the air was filled with the scent of cinnamon and melted butter. I sat cross-legged on the kitchen counter wearing one of Bishop's white undershirts, watching him man the skillet like a pro. A shirtless pro. A shirtless, tattooed, sexy-as-hell pro.

"I have to say that I never expected this. Do you cook other stuff besides French toast?" I could tell he'd made the dish before by the way he expertly kept the bread from being oversaturated with egg. Not always an easy feat.

"With five little brothers and sisters, I learned to cook at an early age. Nothing fancy, but enough to keep everyone fed."

"That makes it sound like the task fell on your shoulders a lot."

He shrugged, flipping the sizzling toast. "Dad passed away when I was seventeen. Ma had to work as much as she could. Wasn't much choice, but it never bothered me too much. Life happens. Resentment would've only made things worse."

Jesus, I'd had no idea.

Why would you? You've never taken the time to learn anything about him.

Ouch. That was a little harsh, if not a tiny bit justified.

"I'm so sorry. I didn't realize."

"That was over ten years ago. Nothing to be sorry about now." He glanced my way and flashed a small smile.

"Can you tell me how he died? If you don't want to talk about it, though, I totally understand." I suddenly realized I was starving to know everything about him.

"No, it's fine. Really. Died of lung cancer. He smoked like a chimney." Bishop stacked the fried bread onto a plate and walked over to me, coaxing my legs to dangle so he could stand between them. "Not crazy about cigarettes because of that. Never touched the things in my life."

My heart clenched tight in my chest for the boy who'd had to grow up too quickly. "I'd say that's understandable. Fortunately, I'm not a fan either." I leaned in and pressed my lips to his, opening when his tongue sought entrance. We kissed languidly for a long minute until my stomach rumbled again. I devolved into a fit of giggles, hiding my face in the crook of his neck.

"All right, kitten. Let's feed you."

Breakfast was delicious—the atmosphere was relaxed and comfortable—but it was the company that made the meal a treat. My attraction to Bishop wasn't just about sex. I truly enjoyed spending time with him. He was funny and thoughtful and open-minded. Conversation with him was effortless.

I wasn't sure where our relationship would take us, but I was certain of one thing. Finding the perfect man right out of the gate might not be such a bad thing. One and done had sounded like a nightmare before I'd met Bishop. Now, I couldn't imagine wanting anyone else.

EPILOGUE

Five Weeks Later

I SHOULD HAVE BEEN TIRED AFTER A LONG DAY OF MOVING, but excitement about having my own place made it easy to wait up for Bishop. I could hardly believe the place was mine. Two bedrooms and spacious but nothing ostentatious. It was absolutely perfect. A part of me kept waiting for someone to walk in from another room and yell at me to get out of their home.

It didn't help that every single piece of furniture in

the place was new. I'd spent the past month outfitting the place, scheduling all the deliveries for the day of closing. I hadn't wanted to wait a minute longer than necessary. Fortunately, all the papers were signed without issue, and I was now a proud homeowner.

Bishop had been so supportive. He'd spent the day helping with my move, then had to run into work at the club for a few hours. That gave me a little time to set up my kitchen and unbox a few things. The amount of crap I'd had to buy almost exceeded the belongings I'd brought from my parents' house. From cleaning supplies to kitchenware to bathroom towels, going out on my own had been a massive endeavor. And it was worth every penny.

And the fact that I would be spending the first night in my new place with Bishop made it all the more sweet. He'd texted to say he was on his way, so I was listening for him when the keypad chimed at the front door.

I jumped up as he let himself in, grinning even wider when I saw the gorgeous bouquet in his hand. "Hey there, handsome."

Bishop flashed his trademark dimples. "I could definitely get used to this." He set down the flowers on the kitchen counter and pulled me in for a kiss that I felt down to my toes. When he pulled back, his warm brown eyes glinted with honeyed caramel. "Security guy is coming tomorrow to install the new system."

"You know there's already excellent security in the building," I pointed out, still smiling.

He simply smirked, telling me he didn't care. I

playfully rolled my eyes, not actually opposed to a security system. I just liked to challenge him sometimes so he didn't forget I could.

"I'd thought about changing clothes before you got here, but once I ended up on the sofa, I couldn't make myself get up." I peered down at the oversized, dirty T-shirt I'd worn all day.

"I'm glad you didn't," he mused, stepping closer.

When I met his stare, the simmering heat behind his eyes summoned a pool of liquid need deep in my belly. "Oh yeah?" I asked, my voice going husky.

Bishop walked me backward until the counter was at my back, then placed his hands on either side of me and brought his lips languidly to mine. Our tongues tangled, slow and ardent. When he finally pulled away, he held a pair of scissors in his hand that had been left on the counter.

I watch raptly as he slid the scissors from the bottom of my T-shirt to the top, cutting it wide open. His eyes gleamed deviously.

"What do you think you're doing?" I breathed.

"Opening my housewarming present."

"That's not how this works. My place, I should be the one unwrapping a gift."

Bishop's answering grin was downright wicked. "Oh, you'll get yours soon enough." He swiftly spun me around and used the shirt remnant to secure my hands behind my back. When he brought me back around to face him, the scissors were in his hand again, and his eyes were locked on my chest.

"Bishop," I warned. "This is a two-hundred-dollar La Perla bra."

He never even flinched. "I'll buy you two in every color." Then he gingerly slipped the end of the shears beneath the delicate lace center, the cold on my heated skin making me gasp and arch. With one firm scissor of the blades, the bra split apart, my breasts spilling out.

"Fuck, *yes*," he growled. His arousal was so damn hot that I couldn't even be mad.

Bishop led me to the new dining table and bent me over it. The cold was a shock against my chest, but I quickly forgot about anything outside of Bishop's hands stripping me of my shorts and panties.

"You're so damn sexy." His hand caressed my ass.

I arched, presenting myself for his pleasure, suddenly feeling desperately empty. "Please, Bishop. I need you inside me."

"I know, kitten. And I'm gonna give you exactly what you need." He angled his hips back to line himself up at my entrance, then pressed forward. One hand continued to caress me while the other took hold of the shirt around my hands and tugged me against him. The movement created a delicious friction as my nipples rubbed against the table.

"Yesss," I moaned.

Bishop picked up speed. He felt so incredible. My inner muscles clenched and contracted in search of more.

"Fuck, baby. You squeeze me like that any more, and I'll never last."

I bit back a smile, squeezing as tight as I could. Bishop's palm slapped my ass, eliciting a delicious burn that had my core weeping.

A few more punishing thrusts, and he yanked off my bindings, then flipped me so that I lay on my back, knees pulled back. I was fully exposed and dripping need.

"God, you're incredible." Bishop stripped off his T-shirt in one swift motion, then dropped to his knees. "And I'm gonna eat you out until those legs fucking quiver."

A man of his word, that's exactly what he did. Then he fucked me so thoroughly that he had to carry me to bed. I wasn't sure my legs were ever going to work again. Not that I cared. He was totally worth it.

◊

THE NEXT DAY was much more leisurely. I spent time organizing and cleaning, then took a nice long nap. I was going to need it because Noemi, Shae, and I were going out for Noemi's twenty-first birthday. She and her husband had already celebrated while on their honeymoon. This outing was just for the girls.

"You ready?" Bishop asked when he came by to pick me up. I'd just applied the finishing touches to my makeup when I heard him let himself in.

"Yeah, let me grab my clutch." I joined him in the living room, loving the way his eyes darkened when he saw me.

"Jesus, you're trying to kill me."

"It's just a basic black dress." I did a little twirl.

Bishop's hungry stare licked down my body. "There is absolutely nothing *basic* about you. Now, let's get out of here before I change my mind and cuff you to the bed."

If my heart inflated any more, I could have floated my way to the elevator.

He was quiet in the car all the way to Noemi's building. I knew he worried about me, so I took out my phone and did something I'd been thinking about doing for a while.

"Let me see your phone," I said once we were parked.

He raised his brows but complied, unlocking it before handing it over. I pulled up the Find Me app, then showed him where my name and location were now listed.

"That help any?" I asked softly. Considering I'd lived all my life with my parents watching my every move, I was more wary than most to give someone access to my movements. That was personal. Private. I didn't want just anyone knowing what I was doing at any given time. But Bishop was different. After thinking about it long and hard, I realized that I wanted him to know. And it made me happy to give that security to him.

"You sure you're okay with that?" He knew how much I prized my independence. The fact that he would ask was exactly why I was willing to share.

"Yeah. I actually kind of like knowing you can find me," I admitted with a smile.

"Fuck, you're cute." His hand cuffed my neck and brought my lips to his. "And yes, it helps a lot. Thank you, baby. Now, text your girl and let her know we're here." Bishop had graciously offered to play Uber for the night. He would have liked to have joined us, even if only to skulk in the distance and observe, but I insisted that this party was girls only.

The three of us ladies unloaded in front of the club thirty minutes later. We looked HOT, if I did say so myself. It was a crisp October night, but that didn't stop us from wearing our hottest clubbing attire. Besides, it wouldn't be an issue once we hit the dance floor.

The club was alive with energy when we arrived—the pumping bass, the gyrating bodies, the flashing colored lights—an intoxicating cocktail for the senses.

"Let's get this party started!" Shae called out, leading us to the bar.

We kicked off the night with shots. How else did you celebrate turning twenty-one? We danced, laughed, and gossiped about the guys with the occasional stop at the bar thrown in. When one hour bled into two, however, I noticed that Shae had grown quiet. And I might have just been drunk, but I could have sworn she'd been nursing the same drink for an hour.

"You okay?" I asked over the music.

Shae's gaze flitted quickly to mine and away. "Yeah, but you two stay here. I'll be right back." She didn't stick around long enough for questions.

Noemi and I turned wide eyes on one another.

"What's up with her?" I asked.

She shrugged. "No clue."

We both turned to watch her and almost fell out of our chairs when she pulled a WWE move that sent a full-grown man to the ground.

"Holy shit!" I blurted while Em stared slack-jawed. Then we both burst from our seats and rushed to Shae's side where she held the man facedown on the ground with one of his arms pulled back at an awkward angle.

"Who sent you?" Her voice was cold as steel. I was so damn impressed.

The man winced but didn't cry out. Instead, he peered up at her, eyes narrowing. "You wouldn't happen to be a Byrne, would ye?" He had a decadent Irish accent that made him sound surprisingly carefree. I couldn't see his features well, but he looked fit, though it had done him little good.

"Depends. Who the hell are you?" Shae shot back.

"Let me up, and I'll tell ye. This isn't exactly the place for a private conversation."

At that moment, two burly bouncers made their way to the front of the spectators circling us. Shae eyed them, then reluctantly allowed the Irishman off the ground.

"Don't even think of disappearing. I want an explanation. Over there." She motioned to our table where our nearly full drinks had been left unattended. It was a shame. I'd have to throw mine out, and it had been nearly full. Though from the look of things, sobering up was a good idea.

The area settled back to its lively status quo. Our

little scene, while harrowing for us, had only been a tasty morsel of entertainment for everyone else. The bouncers still eyed us, ready to escort us out, but everyone else's attention had moved on.

"Who are you?" Shae repeated when we'd all gathered back at the table.

Now that I could see the man in full, I was shocked at how attractive he was. His curly brown hair was artfully messy on top, and the square cut of his jaw was masculine perfection, accented by a neatly trimmed layer of stubble. But it was the line of his angular brow, low over deep-set dark eyes, that stole the show. Together with that accent? There were no words.

"I was sent from Dublin," he answered cryptically.

"And you expect me to believe you didn't know who I was? You've been eyeing us for half an hour, not at all discreetly, I might add."

His teeth pulled at his full bottom lip. "Would ye believe it was a coincidence? I got into town yesterday and was told this was the place to be. I couldn't help but watch ye three. Yer the most beautiful women in the room. Suppose it makes sense now. Irish lasses always have a special kind of wild beauty."

Oh, hell. He was a charmer.

His words might have sounded smarmy coming from someone else, but he made every syllable sound *damn* good.

Shae shifted her weight and crossed her arms over her chest. "I don't believe in coincidences, especially not when you're involved."

"Hey, now. You don't even know me yet. Wait until you've had a drink with me before you write me off." He turned to me and winked. "Now then, what are we celebrating? Whatever it is, I'd say it calls for a toast. I'll even buy the next round."

I shot wide eyes back at Shae, no clue if she'd want this guy gone or kept close to get more information. Her stare was locked firmly on Mr. Dublin. He'd reached into his back pocket then stilled, turning glinting obsidian eyes on Shae.

"Now, lass. Is that any way to welcome a visitor to your fine country?" His voice lowered with a hint of warning. "I'll be taking my wallet back now."

Oh, snap! She'd lifted the guy's wallet in the skirmish. And she didn't look the tiniest bit remorseful.

"If you are who you say you are, I'll be happy to give it back tomorrow when you come by the office." She raised a confident brow.

He chuckled deep and mirthlessly. "I'm afraid that's not going to work for me." The man moved so fast, I didn't know what had happened until it was over. He'd taken her one arm, evaded her attempt to free herself, and somehow twisted her around to seize her other arm, both now tightly secured behind her back. "No need for another scene, lass," he murmured. "I'll just be taking back what's mine." He felt her back pockets with his free hand, unfazed when Shae tried to thrash out of his grip. "Easy, bonny Byrne." His hand came around to pat the empty front pockets of her jeans before pausing at her waist.

"Go after it, and I'll break every one of your damn fingers," Shae said through clenched teeth.

I felt like I was watching a movie unfold. It was captivating and terrifying at the same time. We were surrounded by people, yet none of them had the slightest clue what was playing out.

"You want your wallet, I'll give it to you," Shae growled. "Then you better get the fuck out of here."

The man sighed, lips thinning as though genuinely disappointed. "Never meant to ruffle yer feathers, lass." He freed her arms.

Shae turned to face him with perfect calm and pulled a worn brown leather wallet out from the front of her pants. "Take it and leave. I'll make sure my uncle knows all about your appearance tonight."

He held the wallet up in thanks. "I'm countin' on it." He turned and nodded to Noemi and me. "Ladies."

Then he was gone.

"Ho-ly shit," I drew out slowly. "Who the hell was he?"

The most nefarious, self-satisfied smile I'd ever seen crept its way across Shae's face. She reached into her bra and pulled out an ID. My jaw dropped to the floor. She'd given the man his wallet but made sure to snag the most important part before ever returning to the table.

She set the plastic card pointedly in the middle of the table. "Ladies, meet Devlin McGrath. I doubt it's the last we'll see of him."

♦

Thank you so much for reading SECRET SIN!
The Byrne Brothers is a series of interconnected
standalone novels. The next book in the lineup is
Corrupted Union, which you can read more about
below.

Bonus Epilogue

Before you move on to the next book, I've got one more
taste of Bishop and Pippa for you. The story wouldn't be
complete without a look down the road, so don't miss
this steamy glimpse into the future!

Scan the QR code below or head to my website listed
below for your free download.
www.jillramsower.com/bonus-content/

Secret Sin Bonus Epilogue

Corrupted Union (The Byrne Brothers #2)

Keir Byrne wasn't looking for a wife, but the governor's

daughter is in danger, and a marriage would benefit both of them. The only problem? Rowan is already in a relationship with someone else. Fortunately, Keir isn't the type to let an unwilling bride get in the way of his plans...

Corrupted Union

🔥

Missed the first Byrne Brothers novel?
Check out Silent Vows, in which Noemi must either marry a ruthless Irishman or refuse and face the wrath of her murderous father.

Silent Vows

🔥

Stay in touch!!!

Make sure to join my newsletter and be the first to hear about new releases, sales, and other exciting book news! Head to www.jillramsower.com or scan the code below.

ABOUT THE AUTHOR

Jill Ramsower is a life-long Texan—born in Houston, raised in Austin, and currently residing in West Texas. She attended Baylor University and subsequently Baylor Law School to obtain her BA and JD degrees. She spent the next fourteen years practicing law and raising her three children until one fateful day, she strayed from the well-trod path she had been walking and sat down to write a book. An addict with a pen, she set to writing like a woman possessed and discovered that telling stories is her passion in life.

Social Media & Website

Official Website:
www.jillramsower.com

Jill's Facebook Page:
www.facebook.com/jillramsowerauthor

Reader Group:
Jill's Ravenous Readers

Follow Jill on Instagram:
@jillramsowerauthor

Follow Jill on TikTok:
@JillRamsowerauthor

Made in the USA
Coppell, TX
13 June 2023

18013379R00080